"But I love you," he insisted.

"Love is more than attraction, Brad." Laura smiled gently. "It begins with friendship, compatibility—"

"I think we have that," he replied.

"Then it grows into admiration and respect, where aspirations and values are shared," she continued. "It involves being willing to place someone else's happiness above your own. And I think it's knowing you'd rather be with someone more than anyone else in the world."

She paused and gazed up at him. "Those are the benefits of a sacred commitment. I determined long ago, I'd settle for nothing less."

Brad's gaze darkened. He took her hand.

"What about us?" he asked.

"Only time will tell. You never know what will happen when you regain your memory," she reminded him, her voice husky with emotion.

"There's nothing in this world that could change the way I feel about you, Laura McBride."

DORIS ENGLISH

After only one year in college, Doris English left school to marry her high school sweetheart. Forty years later and more in love than ever, he is still the man of her dreams and she would do the same thing all over again.

Although marriage and children—three daughters—delayed her education and put her dream to write on hold, she nurtured that dream by pursuing her education when she could work it in between family commitments. In 1990, just one year before her youngest daughter graduated from college, Doris graduated from West Georgia University with a 4.0 average and a B.A. in history and a minor in journalism. Meanwhile, she fulfilled her writing dreams by writing articles for inspirational magazines, historical journals, newspapers and inspirational novels.

Doris and her husband, Bob, live on a small farm just outside of metropolitan Atlanta where she delights in sitting on the front porch of her modified French country home and watching deer graze in the pasture in front of her house. They enjoy travel and their cabin in the Blue Ridge Mountains where Doris spends her most productive hours writing.

Doris's message to young women in whose heart God has put a dream is don't despair. Set your priorities in order and God will bring you the desires of your heart.

A Healing Love
Doris English

Love Inspired

Published by Steeple Hill Books™

STEEPLE HILL BOOKS

Steeple
Hill™

ISBN 0-373-87060-4

A HEALING LOVE

Copyright © 1999 by Doris Staton English

Printed in U.S.A.

Therefore if any man be in Christ, he is a new creature. Old things are passed away, all things become new.

—*2 Corinthians* 5:17

To the man of my dreams, my husband, Bob,
whose constant encouragement and steadfast belief
in my dream during the times when I struggled and
doubted, kept me faithful.

Chapter One

Dr. Laura McBride eased her red sports car into the morning rush-hour traffic, headed toward the freeway. Once on the main north-south artery, traffic evened out and the young doctor had time to puzzle over why her former medical school suite mate, Darlene Coleman, had invited her into the city for a visit.

They hadn't been in touch for several years—not since the two had left to do their residencies. When Darlene's unexpected invitation arrived last week, curiosity had drawn Laura like a magnet. A weekend in the city seemed a welcome relief from her duties in her dad's clinic, now a fully accredited hospital located in a quiet hamlet in the foothills of the Blue Ridge Mountains.

The congested neighborhoods of the inner city gave way to larger, towering structures. Laura saw the sprawling new medical center ahead, and beside it Darlene's office complex. A twinge of envy clouded

Laura's countenance. She had rejected a residency at this very hospital to return to her father's small clinic. Her refusal proved Darlene's opportunity.

Laura stepped out of the glass elevator tower into a plush reception room of marble floors, lofty ceiling and a magnificent view of the river. Laura still had trouble visualizing her shy, somewhat stodgy, suite mate managing successfully in such an elite urban environment.

A woman in a tailored navy suit and silk blouse looked up from the reception desk and stared at Laura coolly. She reached a manicured hand behind her for an acrylic pad before asking Laura if she were a new patient.

Laura beamed, ignoring the woman's frosty look. "No. Please tell Dr. Coleman that Dr. Laura McBride is here."

"Dr. McBride?" the woman repeated as she scanned a computer screen. "I don't have you down on her appointment list."

"Nevertheless she is expecting me. Please tell her I'm here," Laura insisted softly but firmly.

"Have a seat, Dr. McBride. It may be a while before Dr. Coleman can see you. She is quite busy you know."

Scarcely five minutes had passed before a svelte blonde with long shiny locks pulled back in a fashionable chignon entered the room. Thick lashes fringed her large doe-shaped eyes. Perfectly applied makeup accented high cheekbones, and bright-red lipstick emphasized a full, sensuous mouth. The cranberry wool-jersey dress she wore caressed her slender, well-contoured figure, and an expensive cameo surrounded by diamonds and seed pearls nestled demurely at her throat.

"Laura, how good to see you," the blond vision said. "You haven't changed a bit."

"Dar-Darlene?" Laura began hesitantly. "Is that really you?"

Darlene's laugh was low, melodious. "A new improved version. A change was long past due for me. You, on the other hand, were always disgustingly perfect."

"You look great!" Laura exclaimed.

"Thank you. I have enjoyed the change. As someone put it—from mousey to peacock."

"No one would ever dare call you 'mousey' again."

"I hope I've put those days long behind me. Now, enough of me. I want to hear about your exciting adventure in that mountain hospital and clinic with your famous dad. Tell me all the details about your work, the hospital, everything, but first give me fifteen minutes to finish seeing my patients and I'm free for the rest of the day."

"You're free this afternoon?" Laura cast a questioning glance toward the receptionist.

Darlene chuckled. "I've blocked out the rest of the day and weekend for you."

Laura finished the last bite of her omelet and reached for a steamy cup of tea. Sitting in a sunny nook of Darlene's kitchen, she relished this last full day in the city. It had been a perfect holiday for her.

They'd attended a concert, dined in a fine restaurant and toured the hospital. The highlight of the weekend had been a lecture by Dr. James McNulty, a renowned endocrinologist. Once again, envy tugged her heart at the opportunity Darlene had working here and being exposed to the cutting edge of medicine. She quickly suppressed the thought, feeling somehow disloyal to her father and the choices she had made years ago.

She was about to ask what their plans for the day were, when Darlene interrupted.

"Laura, why did you choose to go home to help your father, when you could have had all this?"

"You captured this job on the basis of your performance," Laura hedged, ignoring Darlene's question.

"But why did you go back? I saw your eyes when Dr. McNulty was lecturing. You hung on his every word," Darlene pressed, refusing to be diverted.

Laura shook her head, her eyes bright, candid. "Can't deny I enjoyed it, and maybe envied your advantages for a moment, but I chose to go back because it was the right thing to do."

Darlene narrowed her eyes. "Why do you think that?"

"It was something my dad had looked forward to since I was a little girl."

"But what about what you wanted to do?"

"I've just never considered anything else."

"What about your skills, your goals? I'll wager that you live in your father's shadow."

Laura winced; her friend had hit too close to home. Having grown up in and around the hospital, she had yet to prove her mettle as a doctor. To most she was still Doc Dave's little girl, Laura.

Darlene's keen eyes noted Laura's reaction and she pushed her advantage. "It's time to take control of your future. Stop living someone else's dreams."

"Easier said than done," Laura admitted lamely, once again feeling disloyal to her father.

"Why don't you come to work here with me?"

Laura's eyes widened; surprise rendered her speechless.

Darlene laughed. "Things are changing here. There is plenty of opportunity for both of us."

When she found her voice, Laura asked breathlessly, not believing, "You're offering me a job?"

"Maybe a partnership. As you can gather—" Darlene waved her hand around her well-appointed penthouse "—it doesn't come without its advantages."

"I'm overwhelmed," Laura responded, then after a long moment shook her head, something akin to longing briefly flaring in her eyes. "But I couldn't."

"Don't say no until you've met Brad. I've told him all about you. You'll meet him tonight." A knowing smile twitched one corner of Darlene's scarlet mouth. "I haven't met a woman yet who could resist his charms. Even I couldn't. You see—" she hesitated, a flash of uncertainty in her eyes "—we're engaged."

Strains of chamber music from a string quartet greeted Darlene and Laura as they entered Dr. Michael Bradford Jeremiah's lavish apartment perched high above the street facing the river, now a mere ribbon of liquid gold in the departing sun.

People in evening attire gathered in small groups

around the large sunken living room. Laura was glad she had worn her new violet crepe. The dress clung gracefully to her slender body, revealing her feminine curves. Above the deep blue, her eyes sparkled like sapphires and excitement flushed her cheeks. Conversation diminished when the two exquisite blond women entered the room. Laura's hair fell like a cloud in lustrous waves to her shoulders, while Darlene's was caught up in a French twist, held in place with glittering combs.

A tall man with close-cropped dark hair detached himself from a group in the back of the room and made his way toward them. He moved with the grace of a dancer; his broad shoulders looked wide enough to fill a doorway, yet his torso tapered to slender hips. His evening jacket and trousers were tailored perfectly. When he came nearer, the soft light revealed chiseled features a Greek statue could envy. His generous mouth turned up in a smile of greeting as he reached over to kiss Darlene's cheek, but his dark, brooding eyes never left Laura.

When he turned to her, having assessed her, he nodded his approval and observed, "This must be the wonder woman I've been hearing about."

Darlene's smile had a hint of triumph in it as she acknowledged, "The very same."

Laura handed her hand to the ebony-eyed giant and smiled broadly, her cheek dimpled. "Dr. Jeremiah, I'm pleased to meet you."

He exuded charm and confidence with almost a touch of arrogance, yet she detected sadness, a wariness in his eyes, as he inquired, "Well, are you?"

"Am I what?" Laura asked, a puzzled wrinkle in her brow.

"Wonder Woman." He chuckled.

"The last time I looked I was Laura McBride."

"I know. I've heard about you for two years, and of late how much you need to come to Louisville."

"And what was your response to that?" she challenged, lifting her chin a bit.

He laughed. "Guarded. That is, until I saw you walk through that door. Now, I'd say, you have definite possibilities."

Dawn streaked the eastern sky just as Laura reached the interstate. Unwelcome emotions buffeted her as she rushed toward home. Like a forbidden fruit, the memory of Darlene's offer kept playing through her mind. The lure of the city, the opportunities of a modern research hospital, couldn't be denied.

But then there was her father, the clinic and Mark.

Mark! Yes, there was Mark. Capable, wonderful Dr. Mark Harrod, assistant chief of staff, was Dr. David McBride's right-hand man and devoted to Laura. She shook her head attempting to dismiss Mark from the equation that plagued her. She frowned as his dear familiar face smiled from the corridor of her memory, only to be pushed aside by the image of a handsome, dark-eyed giant who whispered, "Well, are you Wonder Woman?"

Thunder rolled across the old heart pine floors, reverberating against the wall and waking Laura from a much-needed afternoon nap. A bolt of lightning illumined the curtained dimness of the room, followed by another peal of thunder and a gust of wind that shook the old farmhouse. Reluctant to move, she gathered the cool, smooth sheets beneath her chin and flinched as the furious storm outside vented its fury.

She closed her eyes and memories of last evening's frenzy matched the rhythm of the squall outside her home. What a homecoming last night proved. No sooner had she reported for duty than she learned that for the first time she was to be left in charge of the clinic, with neither Mark nor her father in calling distance. They had been gone only a couple of hours when a major crisis had occurred.

She chuckled mirthlessly as she remembered her frustration tinged with envy when she had left Darlene yesterday. Driving home, she'd daydreamed of what it would be like to show the clinic that the youngest Dr. McBride had the skill and intelligence to be a competent physician and surgeon.

Her fantasy had become reality too soon. Near panic had engulfed her when Tom Watson arrived on a stretcher, his mangled limbs covered with blood from a logging accident. One look told her there would be no time to wait for assistance. She shuddered. The muscles in her shoulders still ached from the long hours holding a scalpel in her hand while fighting for the injured logger's life.

Her smile broadened. Tom had survived and, without any unforeseen complications, would have only minimal disability. A warm glow spread through her even now as she remembered her dad's arrival and the soft words of praise he spoke. Last night she had met a challenge and passed it with flying colors; now she no longer had to wonder about her ability to respond when the chips were down.

Suddenly, a sense of freedom released the tensions of last night and she sighed with relief and thanksgiving. Throwing back the covers, she hopped out of bed and bounded down the stairs to face the storm with a newfound confidence.

The red-gold boards of the flooring felt smooth and cool to her bare feet as she walked toward the front door of the stately old farmhouse. She tightened her robe around her waist and peered through the leaded-glass window in the massive oak door. The muted afternoon light caressed Laura's face, revealing faint lines of fatigue around her eyes. She pushed against the door and stepped through.

The fierce spring squall that had rolled down from the mountains behind her, depositing a downpour on the valley, had departed as quickly as it had arrived, leaving the air washed sweet and clean. A heavy fog clung to the mountains, shrouding their peaks. Laura breathed deeply and savored the change.

A movement behind interrupted her reverie, and she turned to meet the warm affection in the eyes of her grandfather Jonah McBride. He sat in the oak swing that had been hanging serenely at the end of the porch for as long as she could remember.

She knew he had been watching the storm. ''God's fireworks,'' he called them, claiming it helped a man to be reminded of the Almighty's awesome power, lest he take it for granted.

Now his serene gaze questioned hers and he shook his head.

She explained sheepishly, "The storm awakened me."

"Storm or not, you didn't get enough sleep, Laura," he barked in his gravelly voice.

"Is the doctor diagnosing the doctor?" She grinned, turning one corner of her mouth up, revealing a dimple.

"I don't diagnose since I retired from practice. I'm just speaking as a concerned grandfather to the apple of his eye," Jonah stated, his eyes bright blue under craggy brows. He patted the seat beside him and added softly, "Rough night, honey? Come over here and tell me all about it."

Her smile broadened as she returned the warmth in his eyes. "As if you didn't already know."

"I'd still like to hear the whole story from you."

"Dad told you about Tom?"

"Yes, but mostly he told me about a certain Dr. McBride, third-generation physician. Glowing report. Seems she saved a man's life."

"Not by myself."

"You were the only physician available," he reminded her.

"I thought I really wanted that opportunity and when it came—"

"You found out you were really a doctor," Jonah proposed, an ancient wisdom firing his eyes.

"Yes, I found out, Papa," Laura murmured, more to herself than him.

"And how did it feel?"

"Like sweet relief."

Jonah chewed the side of his lip and raised one eyebrow questioningly.

"I didn't let Dad down," she explained haltingly.

"Is that what's behind all this?"

"How could I ever measure up to everyone's expectations? To most of the people around the clinic, I'm still his little girl playing with stethoscopes. Sometimes I think he still thinks I am."

"Then why did you come back here, Laura?"

"Because I love him, and if I didn't return, who would carry on his work? This clinic was his dream."

"One man can't choose another man or woman's dream. I can't choose for you." He smiled, but sadness turned the blue in his twinkling eyes to gray as he added, "And neither can your dad. I should know. That's what I did to him and it almost destroyed our relationship."

"But his dream is noble and pure."

Jonah chuckled a bitter little laugh, remembering. "Even so, you must find your own destiny, the one God has tailored just for you."

"And what about the clinic? You know how vital it is to these people."

"Then God will send someone else to pick up the mantle if you're not the one."

"Who's to say I'm not?"

"No one except you. Search your heart to find the seat of your reluctance. When you find it you'll have your answer."

"Perhaps I'm afraid of what I'll find," she confessed. Her voice dropped to a whisper.

"And join millions of others who have traded fulfillment for safety and security. You are unique with gifts and dreams fashioned by a loving God just for you. Choose any other game plan and you'll miss the excitement of fulfilling your destiny."

"Sometimes it's easier said than done."

"True. However, life's not about being easy but about being productive," Jonah added with a shake of his head.

"I can be productive here," Laura insisted, not yet willing to reveal her doubts.

"Sure you can."

"Then what do you mean, Papa?"

"That it needs to be your dream and not a lukewarm extension of your father's. I only want for you to know it is here before you commit yourself. So you'll never have to wonder or struggle with regret."

"But how will I know?"

"Know what?"

"The difference between mine and his."

The question hung suspended in air, unanswered, as a muffled roar sounded.

Jonah stood and moved stiffly toward the railing, looking up. He cupped his ear, tilting it upward toward the steady drone.

"Can you see anything, Papa?"

"It sounds like a plane, but who would be foolish enough to fly in this weather? Must be a truck down on the state highway straining up Clingham's Bluff with a heavy load."

Then from directly above the house came the unmistakable whine of an airplane engine.

Laura joined Jonah and the two of them stood transfixed as they watched a small, single-engine plane lose altitude, its bright-red stripes glowing valiantly in the gray afternoon light.

Laura moaned, "He's too low. He'll never clear the mountain."

With one last sputter, the engine died. They stared at the mountain now enveloped in fog, unable to tear their eyes from the little plane hurtling toward disaster. The small craft struggled on, before disappearing into the fog. A few moments later a flash of light pierced the gray shroud, then only silence reigned.

Laura whirled from the porch railing. "Papa," she yelled over her shoulder as she climbed the stairs two at a time. "Call the hospital and tell them we'll need to get a medivac copter from Louisville. I'll saddle Maleeka and go on ahead. It may be a while before they can take off, since that storm is between the city and us.

"But, Laura, what can you do all alone up there?" Jonah protested.

Laura shot her grandfather a mischievous look. "Who was just reminding me what a competent doctor I am?"

Jonah McBride, acquiescing, nodded, a lock of thick white hair falling across his forehead. "Do you think there is a large enough level space for the copter to set down?"

"I believe there is a small plateau near the top," Laura answered, her voice muffled by her closed bedroom door.

Laura had suited up and returned with bag in hand

in record time. Her heart was pounding when Jonah met her at the bottom of the stairs, his deep-blue eyes grave with concern.

"I called the hospital. They'll be ready. Won't you wait for Mark? That trail is pretty treacherous after a storm. You know your mom got stranded on it one time."

Laura smiled reassuringly at her granddad, all the while fighting the temptation to wait for Mark. She knew he had the afternoon off and her father was in surgery. She couldn't risk the wait. Besides, didn't she need to assume more responsibility?

"There's a difference between Mom and me. I know the trail—she didn't."

"Nevertheless, it's not safe to go up there alone. You know what kind of condition it'll be in after that storm."

"Do you think Mark could change the condition of the trail?"

"No, but being a man—"

"I can ride just as well as he can, Papa."

"And doctor, too, but you might need just a little more muscle than you've got." His eyes lingered on her small slender frame.

"We don't have time to wait," she responded gently when she encountered the fear in his eyes. Then she added with more confidence than she felt, "I'll take some extra rope and let Maleeka make up for the muscle I lack. Suit you?"

"I guess it'll have to. I'd give anything if these old legs would let me go up there with you. Maybe if we saddled up Stormy I might make it—"

Laura shook her head at her grandfather. "Dad would have my hide, Papa. Anyway, I need you here to direct the rescue and keep an eye out for my flares. I'll drop some about every quarter of a mile once I get on the mountain, so you can follow my path. You will be more assistance here than on that narrow trail."

"How are you going to get back down?"

"I don't plan to let night catch me up there," she said.

"What if it does?"

Laura shrugged nonchalantly and bent over to kiss her grandfather. "We McBride women seem attracted to that mountain. Don't you worry. I won't be the first one to spend the night up there if I have to."

Her light tone did nothing to reassure Jonah, and he frowned, worry etched in every line of his face. "I don't think that's anything to make light of, Laura. Your mother was lucky she didn't get hurt any worse than she did. You might not fare so well."

"Luck, Grandfather? You know better than that. Mom's destiny awaited her there. Who knows—maybe mine does, too. Anyway, we have no other choice and I could've already had Maleeka saddled by now. Your 'grandfathering' has overcome your medical instincts."

"I just love you so, kitten," he responded, his eyes moist and bright.

"I know, but I'm going to be all right. You just help me and your 'kitten' will be back before you know it," she teased, as a lump in her throat threatened her studied composure. It had been a long time since her granddad had called her by that childhood endearment.

Chapter Two

Laura spoke softly to Maleeka and the bay mare changed smoothly from canter to gallop as if sensing the urgency in the gentle command. For a few minutes her mistress remained tense in the saddle, as images of the disaster somewhere up above her tumbled through her mind.

Once again she was to face an emergency without the reassuring presence of Mark Harrod. She wrinkled her nose slightly at the thought of Mark and smiled. She had come to depend on him as a mentor, friend and adviser. He encouraged her when she was down, teased her unmercifully, yet was always protective of her. Perhaps her grandfather was correct—she had been hiding in Mark's shadow, afraid to trust her own judgment.

Thick pine straw carpeted the trail, while the fragrance of cedar lingered in the air, fresh and clean smelling after the rain. The branches strewn here and there testified to the violence of the brief storm. What if there were larger trees ahead blocking the narrow path higher up the mountain? No need to borrow trouble; she would deal with that if and when she had to.

The broad trail eased up through the forest and she knew Maleeka would make good time for the first few miles. Soon the steady gait of her mare provided a rhythmic therapy. Her shoulders relaxed and her body leaned into her mount, as horse and rider became one.

The magnificent mare sensed the release and thundered through the forest. Gradually, the pure joy of riding pushed aside the memories of Laura's hectic night, and the apprehension of what awaited her on the mountain retreated. For a few brief moments she gave herself completely to this balm of relaxation that could restore her alertness and quicken her reflexes.

Soon the grim line of her mouth eased but the fine lines of fatigue still lingered around her eyes. She closed them for a moment. The wind bathed her face in a refreshing coolness, and her abundant silvery blond hair escaped the scarlet ribbon that loosely bound it, to stream out behind her in wild profusion. Freckles sprinkled her slightly upturned nose and a determined chin hinted of an independent spirit, adding the final touch to a face that was half woman-half child and altogether enchanting.

The mare slowed her pace as the trail narrowed and bent sharply to the right, where it intersected another. They had reached the foot of the mountain. Laura reined Maleeka in and peered upward. The trail's narrow, boulder-strewn surface was muddy and slick from the rain. Even though her mount was a strong,

surefooted Arabian, it would take more than skill to
maneuver up that mountain. She would need a miracle.

She hesitated, weighing her chances; then, unbidden, thoughts of Darlene and her immaculate city
practice tripped through her mind. Had she envied
Darlene's life-style for its excitement? She chuckled
while reaching into her saddlebag to drop her first
flare. At least her grandfather would know exactly
when she had started up the mountain.

About halfway up the steep trail Laura dropped a
second flare. She glanced at her watch. It was 3:30,
roughly four hours until dark, and she had yet to sight
any of the wreckage. If she didn't soon, night would
catch her up here. She shuddered. The thought did
not appeal to her. Squaring her shoulders, she forged
ahead.

As she neared the plateau and her destination, the
path brought her to the very edge of a rock precipice
that plunged to the valley below. She dropped another
flare, knowing Jonah waited anxiously below. Maleeka had to thread her way among boulders, making
each step secure before taking another on the slippery
surface. When Laura attempted to spur the bay on,
the horse would not be hurried. She knew her business was to get her mistress safely up the treacherous
trail.

Thirty minutes later the smell of scorched rubber
wafted through the heavy damp air. The pathway
turned inward, tunneling narrowly through walls of
granite, before it opened onto a plateau in the side of

the mountain. A stream cascaded from above and made its way around the inside perimeter next to a sheer granite wall. Against it rested a smoldering cockpit, nose down in the bubbling stream, and on the natural shelf fifty feet away sat the splintered tail section. Perhaps at the last moment there had been a break in the clouds and the pilot had attempted a landing on the broad ledge.

Laura dismounted and, after grabbing her bag, began a systematic search of the area. Wreckage lay scattered across the rocky terrain, while clothing and papers nestled in the softly swaying sagebrush. Inside the tail section only a shoe and a few books remained, silent evidence that anyone had inhabited the plane.

She left the aircraft and turned to the edge of the plateau. Peering over the side, she looked into a thick band of trees hugging the steep slope. She saw more debris scattered beneath the trees. Stepping into the evergreens, Laura grasped the prickly trunks, and, from one to the next, braced herself as she advanced toward the ledge, scanning for bodies. Several yards away she found a small notepad flung open and face-down, with the initials M.B.J. on the supple calfskin cover. Next to it was a pale-yellow jacket, now smudged with mud, monogrammed with the same initials. But no sign of the pilot. Had he escaped before the explosion? Why had she not found him somewhere on the ledge above?

Laura's foot slipped on the wet foliage and she slid sideways into a stalwart evergreen, ripping her slicker. Rolling over on her stomach, she reached out toward a low sturdy branch to pull herself upright, when she spied a jean-clad leg protruding from beneath a tall bush just above her.

Urgency replaced caution, and she crawled, struggling through the dense undergrowth, oblivious to the vines and limbs catching and pulling at her clothes and hair. Reaching the small broad tree, she grabbed its prickly branches and jerked them back.

A tall angular man lay crumpled on his stomach. One arm was penned beneath him, the other lay flung out above his head, the hand stilled in a groping position. Laura shook her head. Something about the back of the man's head, his broad shoulders, stirred a memory, a vague familiarity that danced just beyond her recall.

With pounding heart, she inched her way under the tree limbs toward him. Finally her hand touched him, then she moved in, positioning herself even with the upper part of his body. Gingerly, she sat up and slid one arm under his chest, while her other braced his shoulder. As gently as possible, she pulled him over. And came face-to-face with the inert form of Dr. Michael Bradford Jeremiah.

She took his limp hand in her icy fingers and detected a vestige of warmth still clinging to his. Frantically, she searched for a pulse. Leaning her face close to his, she felt a faint breath blow against her cheek...

"Oh, Lord, he is alive!" she exclaimed aloud, half in prayer, half in confirmation.

She dropped his hand to tilt back his head and further free his air passage. Then she jerked open her bag. Incredulity lit her face as she pointed her stethoscope to his chest and found a faint and rapid heart-beat. His skin was cold and clammy, partly from the weather but more likely from shock. She needed those blankets. And help. As soon as she could administer the necessary aid she would somehow climb back up the slope to her flares.

The wind moaned through the treetops and she cast an uncertain eye to the heavens. The clouds still lingered, but visibility, at least for now, was adequate for rescue. Still, she must hurry. Darkness came quickly on the mountain.

Cuts and scratches marred his handsome features; dried blood mingled with mud and pine needles clung to his clothes and skin. He appeared different from the debonair socialite she had met only two days before, but there was no doubt in Laura's mind. This was the very same Dr. Jeremiah who could determine her future if she decided to leave the clinic. And Darlene's fiancé.

Laura looked above her. The disturbed ground told a mute story of his tumble from the plateau above. He had probably pulled himself to the edge and rolled over, trying to escape the plane before it erupted in flames. He was lucky the dense bush had stopped his fall; whether or not it had saved his life still remained to be seen.

She completed her examination. His wounds appeared superficial; however, she suspected his leg was broken, probably in more than one place, as well as some ribs. He had a large knot on the back of his head where dried blood matted his thick dark hair.

As gently as possible she straightened his leg and

brought his arm down to his side, but he made no movement. He was deeply unconscious, or the severe pain would have evoked some response. After taking sterile pads and alcohol from her bag, she bathed his face and with deft hands raised his head slightly to dress his wound.

Now she could leave him briefly for the climb up to the plateau above. Backing out of the bush, she sat on her heels, still holding the prickly branches in her hand. Pausing, she glanced at her patient. His damp hair clung to his forehead in dark curls, and his features, even with his eyes closed, were ruggedly handsome. His still form had a vulnerability about it that provoked a strange tenderness in Laura.

She remained rooted to the spot in front of his long, lean, muscular body, while questions rioted through her mind. What had prompted his flight to this area in this weather? Could he survive? What if he didn't? Unwittingly, a deep sorrow burdened her heart, almost as if she were contemplating a personal loss.

She shook her head, puzzled at her strange response in this quiet stillness. Had her cool physician's objectivity deserted her? she mused, just as the wind whipped a prickly branch into her hair, stinging her neck. She took a deep, calming breath and the physician in her once again resumed control.

Turning from him, she pushed her way, slipping and sliding, back up the embankment, where she retrieved blankets and discharged three flares—the signal there was a survivor. After setting emergency markers for the helicopter, she rushed back to her patient. Just as she reached him a small boulder dislodged beneath her feet and she fell, rolling down the steep slope, straight toward the sheer cliff below them.

Clutching the blankets in one arm, she groped wildly with the other for something to slow her descent. Blond hair and pine straw mingled in a matted mass. Her shoulders and legs painfully impacted rocks, but at last she grabbed on to a tree that held her, stopping her fall.

She sat up slowly, stunned for a moment, then winced as she touched her shoulder. She raised her arm; it moved with only minimal pain. Next she flexed her fingers. Amazingly, she seemed to have nothing more serious than a few scratches and bruises. She glanced hesitantly beyond her feet, where dense evergreens gave way to air, and shuddered. Ten more feet and Brad Jeremiah would have been alone on the mountain.

Laura's mouth tightened into a grim line as she forcefully pushed the fearful "what might have beens" aside. Stoically, she turned and began her climb back up to her patient, this time pulling herself from tree to tree while pushing her supplies before her.

After what seemed like hours but in reality was only minutes, she arrived at Brad Jeremiah's side, to find his condition unchanged. He was still unconscious, and his breathing remained shallow.

She brushed the dirt and straw from the blankets and rolled them tightly to pillow each side of his head. Unable to assess fully his injuries, Laura knew that one jerk of his head, given a severe spinal injury, could put him beyond a surgeon's help.

A few rays of afternoon sun filtered through the brush and Laura looked up gratefully. The light came from low on the horizon, but maybe the rescue crew could make it before nightfall. By the time Laura finished taking his vital signs again and administered what aid she could without moving him, the late-afternoon air had turned cool. She shivered, and realized that her patient must be cold, also.

After removing her bright yellow slicker, she covered him with it. As she placed the soft flannel lining around him, he stirred. Putting a hand lightly on each of his shoulders, she leaned in, her face close to his. Eyes like two small slits opened slightly.

Laura's heart lurched as her eyes encountered his. Even now, a commanding power emanated from the ebony pools.

"Where—where—" He tried to speak, but his mouth was dry and his tongue seemed too thick to form any more words.

"Please lie still. You have had an accident. Your injuries don't appear to be life threatening and assistance is on the way." Laura spoke slowly, distinctly, while attempting a reassuring smile.

"What h-happened?" he persisted as his tongue stiffly formed the words. His eyes, showing no hint of recognition, burned into hers.

"Your plane crashed and you are on Boulder Mountain. A helicopter will be here to get you soon."

"Crashed?" His eyes widened, and he struggled against the gentle pressure of Laura's hands.

"Turn loose," he commanded.

She smiled tightly and answered in a firm voice, without releasing her hold, "Until you are thoroughly checked out, you mustn't move. Help will be here soon."

"Who are you?" he asked weakly, gazing up at her beautiful image; her mud-smudged face and thick, golden locks, windblown and irrepressible.

"I'm Dr. Laura McBride from the Appalachian Clinic a few miles from here, Dr. Jeremiah," she answered softly.

He closed his eyes and remarked, "No, wood nymph."

He raised his hand in a helpless gesture, then his body relaxed beneath her grip. He had lost consciousness again. Once more Laura attached the blood pressure cuff to his arm. The gauge confirmed her fears: his pressure was falling. Help must arrive soon, for there was little else she could do for him. Placing her patient's hand in hers, she waited for their rescuers.

The distant whir of a helicopter broke the stillness and jerked Laura from the lethargy that had claimed her. She had not realized how weary she was from the events of the past two days. Now her body moved reluctantly from fatigue.

A grim smile parted her lips. *That ought to be some ride back down the mountain as sore and stiff as I am.* She winced mentally as she thought about Maleeka patiently waiting for her.

A moan from her patient interrupted her anxious speculation and she put a cool hand to his forehead.

Where it had been cold and clammy earlier, it was now warm with fever.

She whispered a prayer of thanks as the distant whir changed to a deafening roar. The trees overhead blew briskly as the chopper came to rest smartly between the red glowing markers.

"Haaalloooo, Laura. Where are you?" a familiar voice called from above.

Relief flooded through every fiber of her being when she recognized Mark Harrod's voice.

"Here, Mark. And hurry. We need a stretcher and splints. But take care—the slope is very slippery."

The warning had hardly been issued before Mark's tall lean frame stood beside her. He took one look at her and, seemingly oblivious to the man prostrate on the ground, reached one long arm out and pulled her to him, enfolding her in his warm embrace, as he scolded softly, "Don't you ever pull a stunt like that again. You wait for help next time!"

He placed his hand beneath her chin and raised her face, really looking at her for the first time. His pleasant face creased with concern. His hand moved upward to caress the cuts and scratches on her face.

"What happened to you?" he asked worriedly.

"Just banged up a bit, nothing serious. I kinda took a fall...."

"Down this embankment?" Mark all but shouted. "It ends in the valley below via Clingman's Bluff."

"But I didn't end up there. Please, Mark, don't waste time with me. He's the one who needs your attention." Her voice rose with anxiety for her patient.

"That's all right, Laura. I'll attend to him. Let Mark take care of you," said a deep voice behind them.

Laura stood on tiptoe and peered over Mark's shoulder, straight into the twinkling blue eyes of her father. The blood rushed to her face, tinting it scarlet. David McBride's eyebrows raised quizzically as he took in his daughter firmly entrenched in the arms of his chief surgeon.

She pushed harder against Mark's embrace, breaking free of the pinioning arms. "I said I'm *all right!*" she insisted.

"You don't look all right. Sit down and let me dress those wounds. I don't want that gorgeous face scarred," Mark commanded as he stooped to open his bag.

"Don't patronize me, Mark. Just because I'm a woman you think I need pampering." She railed irrationally, embarrassment and fatigue taking their toll.

The young doctor glanced up, his eyes lingering on her beautiful, defiant face. She stood there glaring at him with her hands on her hips and her lips pursed uncharacteristically.

Now that he was certain she was safe, amusement danced in his warm brown eyes and he drawled, "Well, my pretty maid, I'll have to admit it would be mighty hard for me to forget you're a woman." Then he added softly, "Now or anytime."

Laura couldn't deny the message in his eyes, the tone of his voice. It melted her stubborn resistance, and the hint of scarlet on her cheeks deepened. She stammered, "O-okay, if you insist, but I'm not hurt."

"I do insist, and you are hurt as well as on the verge of total exhaustion. It's a good thing I got back in time to come with your father. He'd have had his hands full trying to look after both of you."

"Now, Mark—" she began, her eyes snapping.

"You're right there, Mark," the older doctor agreed. His face was serious and the twinkle gone from his eyes as he observed quietly, "This young man's condition is touch-and-go. He may have some internal bleeding. His blood pressure has fallen some more. Were there any other survivors?"

Laura shook her head. "No. I searched this area thoroughly."

"Were you able to get any information from him?"

"He opened his eyes once, but he was delirious— talked about wood nymphs!" Laura said as the two men stared at her, before both simultaneously burst into laughter.

Laura frowned. "I'm afraid I fail to see any humor in that."

Her father chuckled. "I'm sure that it must have caused him some anxiety that a wood nymph was administering first aid to him."

Laura shot him a sharp look before replying, "How did you know that?"

"That's what you look like—some wildly beautiful forest creature," Mark explained as he reached out and picked up a lock of her hair cascading down her back.

"I must be a sight. Perhaps I should request that the pharmaceutical company design a medical bag equipped with beauty supplies just for women doctors," she teased, all former traces of irritation gone.

"I'll have to disagree with that. I think this 'new' you is enchanting," Mark added, his eyes perfectly serious.

"Thank you, Dr. Harrod. You're a true friend as usual, but dreaming or not, our patient wasn't so injured that he relished being treated by a woman doctor."

"So that's what got your ire up, and you took it out on poor little old me," Mark countered.

"What are friends for if we can't take out our frustrations on them and they still love us, right?"

"You couldn't be more right, my dear," the young doctor responded.

And Laura recognized the same look that she had earlier seen lighting his eyes.

For a moment the two stood staring at each other, Mark's brown eyes immersed in her bright-blue ones. Laura stirred, uncomfortable with the raw emotion displayed in the gaze of her friend, who was usually so casual and congenial.

David spoke, breaking the spell. "He's ready to go to the clinic now, and from my observation, not a moment too soon."

The three doctors stood aside as two medics hoisted the stretcher and passed them on the short treacherous upward journey to the waiting helicopter.

The older doctor reached out and put an affectionate arm around his slender daughter. "You did a good job, Dr. McBride."

She wrinkled her nose, a warm glow returning the

affection in his eyes, "Thank you, Dr. McBride. Wish I could've done more."

"You may well have saved his life. For sure if you hadn't found him when you did, his chances of survival would have been slim. How does it feel saving two lives in twenty-four hours?"

"We're not out of the woods yet," she reminded him softly.

"That's true, but without you there'd be no hope for this young man or Tom Crews last night."

Laura's eyes grew bright with unexpected tears. "That is what it's all about, isn't it, Dad? To save lives, to give people a chance at a better life?"

"Yes, honey. At least to me, that's what all the work and study are about. To have you here with me, sharing my dream, fulfills my deepest hope."

Dropping her head, she murmured, "I know, Dad. I know."

Mark interrupted, "Okay, you two, it's time we tried our luck at climbing that bank. Think you can make it, Laura?"

A glance at Mark assured her that the familiar, comfortable friend she knew had returned, and the uneasiness left her face. She smiled at him impudently. "What are you talking about, Dr. Harrod? I've been up and down that bank—I'm a pro."

"But this time would you forgo your tumbling exercises? We really don't have time for that!" Mark teased.

"All right, Doctor. That's enough. I only tumbled when I came down—not going up!" She flashed a smiling response to his good natured teasing.

Mark's easygoing personality always provided just the right amount of lighthearted repartee when she took life or herself too seriously. But she also depended on him for the strength and compassion that lay beneath his casualness. She valued his friendship as much as she did his professional skill.

Today was the first time Mark had addressed her with an endearment, but it was not the first time she had seen him, in an unguarded moment, look at her with something more than friendship in his eyes. In the past it had lasted only a moment, quickly veiled by his charming nonchalance. She had pushed it aside, not wanting to encourage or deal with it. She preferred his friendship—needed it, in fact. Theirs had been a comfortable relationship, one she wanted to remain as it was, at least for the time being.

They maneuvered up the embankment without incident, except for the resistance of Laura's aching body. Soon they stood at the edge of the clearing, waiting for the medics to load the stretcher.

"I'll ride Maleeka back, and you get in the copter with your dad—that is, if you won't think I'm disparaging you because you're a woman," Mark teased.

Laura grimaced. "Did I really act that ugly?"

"Yeah, pretty ugly, but I'll survive. It was momentary hysteria brought on by fatigue and exposure to the elements, not to mention the absence of one Dr. Harrod. I picked a busy time to leave, didn't I? Did you note I said nothing or even suggested you were a hysterical woman?"

"Yes, Dr. Harrod and I wholeheartedly agree with your diagnosis, but are you sure you can handle that little mare and get back down the mountain before dark?''

"No doubt about that. David, do you think you can manage things until I can make it back to the clinic?'' Mark asked half authoritatively, half teasing.

David chuckled, his eyes merry. "I don't think we have any choice. Our cowgirl here needs some medical attention herself, and I don't know if this aging frame is up to that wild ride down the mountain. No, I guess I'll just have to do the best I can until you can get there.''

Both younger doctors burst into laughter. David McBride's physical prowess at midlife was greater than men half his age. His broad shoulders rippled with muscles and his narrow hips and flat abdomen testified to the vigorous physical activity that he enjoyed every day. In fact, only the sprinkling of silver through his hair and the deepening laugh lines at the corners of his vivid blue eyes and mouth showed his years. Dr. David McBride was a handsome man, and a commanding presence both physically and emotionally. His eyes glowed with an inner strength and his carriage proclaimed him a man who knew himself and was at peace with that knowledge.

Laura had inherited her thick blond hair and deep blue eyes from her father, her fragile frame and other facial features from her mother, but her eyes glowed with her very own inner beauty that mingled with an innocent curiosity about life. The promise of strength was there and would come later when she found those answers.

Without warning, a total weariness washed over

her, and, too tired to continue their bantering, she agreed, "Thank you, Mark. I'll owe you one."

He twisted his face in a mock, leering glare. "Never you fear, my lovely. I'll collect."

As soon as Laura and David were airborne, Mark started down the long trail toward the sprawling Victorian farmhouse where an anxious Jonah McBride paced up and down the old front porch.

Chapter Three

A bright midmorning sun streamed in through the leaded-glass window as a gentle breeze wafted through the open casement, stirring the lace curtains. From outside, the soft whinny of horses and the metallic clang of feeding buckets told Laura that she had overslept.

Bolting upright in bed, she gave one short yelp as pain coursed through her head in throbbing crescendos. She raised her small scratched hands and pressed her temples. The room receded in darkness for a moment, then slowly refocused.

One foot slid from beneath the satin coverlet and testily reached for the floor. Now her muscles joined her aching head in a painful refrain. She managed to sit up and bring the other foot to rest on the floor, then paused to let the recurring darkness subside once more.

After arising stiffly, she shuffled to the window, a

grimace of pain contorting her features. Standing beside the window, she let the refreshing breeze bathe her face and waited for the pain to diminish. It finally eased.

Outside, Jonah stood, one leg propped up on the split-rail fence, rubbing Maleeka's head and gazing out toward the mountain partially covered by a morning mist. She knew he was reliving yesterday and the terror he'd felt before he saw her safe and sound again. He had been waiting at the hospital when the medivac copter had returned.

She smiled. What a blessing to have a grandfather to love. In fact, what a fortunate woman she was to have a family like hers. Why would she ever want to leave this place? And yet, would she?

She limped toward the bathroom, eager to sink her sore, aching muscles into the large oversize tub supported by stately claw feet. After filling it almost to the top, she settled into the warm water, the fragrance of a spring bouquet teasing her nostrils. She soaked, letting the gentle warm pressure soothe her aching muscles, and soon even the throbbing in her head had decreased to a dull ache.

The staccato of the phone rent the air as she put the large towel around her wet locks, turban style, and fastened a long white terry robe securely around her waist.

"Dr. McBride here," she softly answered. A twinkle lit her eyes and the corners of her mouth curled in a half smile when the familiar voice of her father sounded on the other end.

"How are our patients?" was her eager response.

"Don't you think I'd better come in and relieve you? You've been up for the most part of two nights yourself," Laura reminded him as she heard the fatigue in his voice.

"Oh? Mark's coming in. They'll be in good hands for sure. Yes, sir, I'll take doctor's orders. Rest until three, eat a light breakfast and drink plenty of fluids. See? I am a good patient. Love ya, too. Bye, now."

She replaced the phone on the bedside table, an affectionate smile brushing her lips. She was a "daddy's girl," no doubt about it. Her long fingers gently toweled her hair, as her mind tripped back over the years. Although she loved her parents equally, it was her father's approval that had motivated her to excellence. In fact, if she faced the truth, it was he who had influenced her career choice. What would she have been were her father just an ordinary man?

A rap on the door interrupted her musings.

Jonah asked from the hall, "You decent, honey? I've got some coffee for you."

"You old sweetheart. I was coming down for it," she protested, leaning over to kiss him on his weathered cheek once he'd entered.

"Let me pamper you a little. Isn't that what grandparents are for? Since I'm the only one you have, I get to do it twice as much." He winked at her even as a shadow of wistfulness touched his eyes.

"You still miss Grandmother, don't you?"

He nodded. "And I will until I draw my last breath."

"But it's been so long."

"Forty years. I had her for only twenty, but that

was long enough to know there'd never be another for me. Some people love like that. God blesses them with such a perfect love that no one else can replace it."

"You didn't ever date after she died?"

He chuckled. "Sure. People tried to fix me up all the time. Believe it or not, I was quite a catch in my day."

"You don't have to convince me. I think you're still a catch. But no one could live up to Grandmother?"

"No, it wouldn't have been fair to someone else. When you've had the best, you can't accept second best. I'd always been comparing and they could have never met my expectations, so I've settled for my memories."

"Good ones?"

"Some wonderful ones, but some regrets, too."

"Regrets?" Laura asked, puzzled.

"Regrets that I spent too much of my time and energy building a successful urban practice. Time I took away from my Anna. I thought we'd have plenty of time later when I got my work established. It didn't work out that way." He turned his piercing blue eyes on Laura and added, "Don't ever put relationships on hold, Laura. Savor them. You never know the future."

"Do you think Grandmother had regrets?"

A deep sadness touched Jonah's eyes before he answered her, then he nodded. "Disappointments, too, probably, but she never voiced them to me."

"Why?"

Jonah sighed, a sad little smile tugging at the corners of his mouth. "Because she had learned to savor the times that we did have together and refused to let anything tarnish their splendor. That's why I have so many wonderful memories, kitten."

"I'm sorry I never knew her."

"You look an awful lot like your grandmother."

"I thought I looked like my dad."

"You do, but you're a lot more delicate. He resembles her."

"Her picture is so beautiful, but it's almost ethereal. I don't see myself like that."

"You do have her golden beauty, but you're right. Yours is not an unearthly quality. You're spunky like your mother."

"Spunky? What do you mean by that?" Laura was puzzled as she visualized her small, dark-haired mother with large indigo eyes.

"Sometimes you have a show-me attitude, and you're always ready to speak your mind."

"You think mom's got a show-me attitude?" Laura arched an eyebrow questioningly. Her grandfather's statement surprised her. He had always loved and admired his daughter-in-law. Was there a veiled criticism in his remark?

"It's mellowed over the years to one of strong conviction, but when she's convinced she's right, there is no stopping her. She speaks her mind in no uncertain terms."

"That's for sure," Laura agreed. "But isn't that part of being a good writer—being a communicator? That's why she's had a successful career, even though she chose to remain here in this rural area. I've wondered lately why she stayed here. When I was younger I just took it for granted, but lately…''

"She's a gifted woman, but one who set her priorities in order.''

"As I think back, she never seemed to struggle with balancing a home and a career,'' Laura observed thoughtfully as she held the steaming cup of coffee in both hands, savoring the aroma before she put it to her lips.

"She struggled with that decision before she married your dad. First she came to terms with what the Good Lord wanted her to do with her life. Then the rest fell into place.''

"Easier said than done.'' Memories of Darlene's tempting offer haunted her for a moment.

"I didn't say it was easy. What's right is rarely easy. When your mom decided to marry your father and stay here, she thought her career was over. In fact, her publisher fired her, but God just brought more and better opportunities here.'' Jonah's eyes misted as he remembered.

"How so?'' Laura's interest was piqued.

"When your mom sacrificed her goals, her ambitions and her ability for what she knew God wanted from her—marriage, a family and living in this rural mountain valley—He gave them back to her enhanced with new opportunities.''

Laura pressed her grandfather, not quite convinced. "You don't think she would have been successful in New York? Her talents were the same. There is opportunity there.''

"She would have enjoyed a measure of success because of her extraordinary talent, but God put her here, where there was a rich field of ideas. Not only did she achieve personal achievement and international recognition, but she was able to make a positive impact on other lives. She would never have had the knowledge or opportunity in New York."

"Do you think God is interested in everyone's life that much, or was Mom just special?"

"Your mom's pretty special, but I believe God is interested in all His children's lives. If He loves us and is our Father, then how could He not be? Do you not think He's interested in your plans?"

"Um, perhaps. To tell you the truth, I've not thought much about it. I'd always planned to be a doctor, and since Dad's destiny was here, I just assumed that I was to follow in his footsteps. That is, until lately." Laura dropped her eyes and her voice, fearing she'd revealed more than she had intended, actually more than even she was ready to admit to herself.

Her grandfather looked at her steadily, then smiled slightly, before commenting dryly, "Sometimes distinguishing between God's will, our will and somebody else's is difficult. But if you achieve the fulfillment you need, you'll have to come to terms with why you are working here with us. Are you trying to fulfill someone else's vision for your life or the destiny God has ordained for you? Only by following God's destiny can your life accomplish its highest purpose."

"You don't think I can attain my goals working with Dad?"

"First you have to define your goals and determine if they're your God-given goals or your dad's."

"Dad never put any pressure on me to come back here," she defended too quickly.

"He wouldn't knowingly. But sometimes children subconsciously pattern their lives after their parents' in an effort to win their approval. This is especially true if they admire them."

Laura turned from her grandfather before he could see the uncertainty his words had stirred in her. She dropped onto her chaise nestled in the alcove, where the morning sun streamed in, then looked up into her grandfather's eyes, a resolute smile on her lips that didn't quite reach her eyes. "I think I'm quite comfortable with my situation—helping Dad and Mark at the clinic, seeing Mom every day and living here with you. Really, who could want more?"

"Comfortable? Hmm." Jonah stroked his chin pensively before adding, "But are you fulfilled?"

The acrid smell of disinfectant greeted Laura as she entered the hospital, and the familiar rush of adrenaline pumped her heart faster. To be even a small part of God's healing process always excited her. Today was no different. Here, she could forget the nagging questions Jonah had stirred, the brief disloyal yearnings she had felt in Louisville. Wasn't it enough to serve in this great field of medicine? Did it matter where, so long as she did?

"Hi, Doc Laura! We didn't expect to see you today. Figured you'd be all tuckered out after yesterday," Francie Dunwoody greeted the young doctor in a familiar Appalachian drawl that identified her as a local.

"I'm stiff but moving, Francie. Would have been tempting to stay put today, but I didn't want to miss out on any excitement." Laura smiled, accustomed to the almost maternal interest the staff took in her. She knew that behind her back they often speculated about her and Mark's relationship, but as yet none had been so bold as to broach the subject with her.

"Your dad just went up to see the new patient. He's got everybody buzzing. How he ever survived that crash is a real mystery. You know..." She chattered on as Laura walked briskly down the polished hallway with a wave of the hand, smiling as she compared Francie's down-home chatter with the cool diction of Ms. Brown of Metropolitan Surgeons and Associates. Sometimes Francie definitely talked too much, but when people were distressed she was a godsend at encouraging and comforting them. Come to think of it, Laura would take Francie's warm jabber over Ms. Brown's frosty competence any day.

Laura took the stairs two at a time, sore, aching muscles forgotten. Arriving at her office a good half hour before shift change, Laura felt a new confidence and contentment. She grabbed her white jacket and slipped it over her navy turtleneck and denim skirt.

Looking in the mirror, she laughed aloud at her image. Francie is not the only "down-home" employee in this hospital. With that she twisted her blond cloud of lustrous curls into a ponytail and tied it with a red-and-blue gingham ribbon. She looked little more than a teenager as she raced out the door toward ICU, where Tom Watson and Dr. Brad Jeremiah resided in adjoining rooms.

Picking up Tom's chart, she noted Brad's was missing. Her father or Mark must be with him. She ducked her head into Tom's room, where Joan Johnson, head nurse on the surgery wing, intercepted her. "Dr. Laura, your dad wants you in temp ICU right away. Dr. Mark is already with him."

Laura heard low masculine voices as she let herself into the sterile pale-green room where two floor nurses checked charts by a desk lamp. The overhead lights were dim and the blinds drawn, shutting out the bright afternoon sun and the glorious view outside the window of the deep narrow gorge that was Thunderbolt Canyon.

The room was sparsely furnished. With only the necessary equipment, it served as a temporary ICU unit when the primary unit was filled to capacity. The need for additional room in surgery and research had reached a critical stage, but so far the elder Dr. McBride had not found sufficient funding to finance the expansion plans. What a far cry this was from the streamlined, well-equipped units she had visited with Darlene. But then, funding proved no problem for Darlene's clinic. Yet, did these patients deserve any less?

She moved the curtain aside, stepped in beside Mark and met the steady gaze of her father. Laura's heart lurched.

"Dad?" she asked a little breathlessly. "Joan said you needed me."

He lifted his head, the light catching silver threads in his hair. Lines of fatigue etched his eyes and mouth. Laura's heart pounded harder.

"I do. Mark and I both have appointments and will be leaving shortly. I've opted to keep the patient in ICU until tomorrow."

"How is he?"

"About the same—his vital signs are stable, but he hasn't regained consciousness yet."

"Is he still sedated from the surgery?"

"Yes, but we don't know whether it's that or…"

"Or what?"

"He's unresponsive from his injury."

"From a broken leg?" Laura questioned.

"His injuries proved a little more complicated than we thought. After Mark finished, inner cranial pressure started building up and we had to go in to relieve it. Now we're just waiting to see what damage, permanent or temporary, was done."

Laura's heart sank. How would the arrogant Dr. Jeremiah cope with news that he could very well have a permanent disability? "What is the prognosis?"

"We won't know until he regains consciousness, and that's where you come in. I'd like for you to stay with him. There is a possibility that we might have to go in and relieve the pressure again, so he needs careful observation and a doctor on duty, just in case."

"Sure thing. I guess you've written everything I need to know on the chart."

"Not quite. There's a matter of just how much damage may have occurred."

"Then you're sure there is damage?"

"Too much blood for there not to be, I fear."

Laura nodded in agreement. "If a third surgery is required will one of you be available?"

"No, my dear, you're it. Dr. Merritt is on standby to assist you if needed."

She shuddered and remembered Darlene. "Dad, do you think I should get in touch with Darlene?"

"Whatever for, Laura?"

"To tell her about Brad."

"Brad? Brad who?"

"Brad Jeremiah. Your patient."

"You know him?"

"Didn't I tell you?"

"Tell us? No! We've worked all night trying to find out this young man's identity so we could contact his family—we needed permission to operate. Finally, we could safely wait no longer and went ahead. If he survives with a permanent disability, no telling what kind of liability that will incur. But I felt I had no other choice," David McBride explained, the impatience with his daughter bordering on anger.

Laura dropped her head before her father could read the dismay in her eyes. "I guess I wasn't thinking clearly last evening. We were so busy in the copter, and then later I went home. Until this moment I didn't realize I had not told you who he is. I'm so sorry."

David sighed. "What matters now is who this Brad

Jeremiah is and if we can get in touch with the family.''

"His name is Dr. Michael Bradford Jeremiah, and he's a physician in the same practice with Darlene. I met him briefly Sunday night at his apartment."

Mark quirked an inquisitive brow in her direction.

Laura blushed and stammered, "I-it was a party with some of Darlene's associates. She took me there."

Mark drawled, trying to lighten the moment, "I didn't know you went to Louisville to go a-partyin' at some rich and handsome doctor's digs. I'd have canceled your leave."

"Did you meet his family or do you know where we can get in touch with them?" David bristled, his brows drawn together, the stress of the past two days showing.

"No, sir. Only Darlene. I'll call her. She should know." Laura's answer was clipped.

"Then call her."

"How much shall I tell her?"

"About the accident, of course."

"How about his injuries?"

"Injured but stable, and we won't know the extent until he regains consciousness. Ask how we can contact his family," the older McBride snapped, then he wheeled on his heel and left the room.

Silence reigned for a few awkward moments, then Mark whistled. "Got his hackles up, I guess."

"He was right. I did drop the ball," Laura admitted, troubled.

"I don't think that's what's wrong with him. I

think he's exhausted, and this beating the bushes for funds is not a role that suits him. As for yours truly, I kinda like it. It's a challenge getting these folks to part with their money. In fact, the two committee men I met with yesterday are coming tonight to tour the hospital. That research grant will be ours if they give the go-ahead. Now how do you like that for my power of persuasion, my young Dr. Mac?" he teased, trying to take her mind off her confrontation with her father.

"I would never doubt your powers of persuasion, Dr. Harrod. Can anyone withstand your Irish charm?" Laura responded, looking up directly into his eyes, a ghost of a smile struggling to emerge.

Mark lifted his eyebrows, questioningly. "Hmm. How about you, Laura?" His voice teased, but his warm brown eyes grew serious.

Laura dropped her eyes, reluctant to go on to the next phase of their relationship. Her heart lurched at the thought of loosing her carefree give-and-take with Mark. It wasn't that she couldn't love Mark. He was everything she wanted in a man. He was sensitive and caring, a man of strong character and principle. He was handsome and fun to be with, and above all they enjoyed a shared faith and dedication to their work. Yet for some strange reason she wasn't ready for that ultimate commitment.

Laura lifted her head, forcing her emotions under control, and winked at him. "I'll never tell, for then you might have me in your power."

Mark clicked his heels together and with a mock bow responded, "I shall live in anticipation of that day."

"Now, if you two have finished clowning we'll attend to the patient," David McBride said as he strode through the door, charts in hand.

Laura turned toward him, to see his dear, one-sided grin aimed at her. The familiar twinkle in his eye told her that all was forgiven, and she breathed a sigh of relief.

Darlene had taken the news of Brad's accident in stride. Giving Laura the name of his mother, who was somewhere in Delaware, she promised to come as soon as possible. Two of the physicians on staff at Medical Surgeons were away, and with Brad's absence, Darlene's workload prevented her from leaving on a moment's notice.

Meanwhile, Laura would contact Brad's mother and hold the fort until Darlene could arrive. She fervently hoped that the patient would be much improved before that. But her father's concern lay like a heavy weight on her shoulders. What would be the aftereffects of Brad Jeremiah's accident? And if there were any, how would he adjust? She drew in a ragged breath and prayed that his consciousness would soon return. Only then would they know what he faced and their part in his recovery.

Now for the unpleasant task of phoning his mother.

Her call proved fruitless. She was an invalid in a rest home on the Chesapeake Bay. The officials there would not allow Laura to speak to her, and said they would relay the message. A sense of lonely frustration swept over her. Drawn like a magnet to his room, Laura returned time after time to stand by his side, willing him to open his eyes, but to no avail. His condition remained unchanged, his breathing steady but labored, his other vital signs stable.

Imagine being confined to a hospital, with serious injuries and no loving family huddled around. She suddenly felt a great empathy for this man she hardly knew. She shook her head, trying to regain a physician's objectivity. But she couldn't. Until Darlene arrived, she was the closest thing Dr. Brad Jeremiah had to family or friend. And so she waited as anxious as any loved one. Fearful he wouldn't awake, and even more fearful of what faced them when he did.

Chapter Four

Midafternoon Laura went to her office to take a shower, hoping it would revive her from what felt like a drowsy stupor that was no doubt a lingering effect of the powerful sedative Mark had administered the night before. She kept a change of clothes in her closet for just such emergencies. She put on a softly feminine blue blouse and navy skirt, this time opting to leave her hair down. It billowed like a soft blond cloud around her shoulders. The mirror reflected her pale face as she carefully applied blush to her cheeks. The long, luxurious lashes framing her vivid blue eyes needed little mascara, just as her near-perfect complexion needed no makeup. Finishing up with a little color on her lips, Laura remembered Mark's appointment and was glad she had changed from her denim skirt. If the prospective donors toured the hospital she wanted to present a professional image.

For the moment Laura felt refreshed, but she

dreaded the long hours of limited activity, fearing her lethargy would return. She returned to Brad Jeremiah's room to begin the long vigil again.

Several hours elapsed before she left him to check on Tom Watson and grab a bite to eat in the staff dining hall, after instructing the nurses to page her the moment they detected any change in the patient. Just as she was finishing her coffee, the PA announced her number, directing her to the surgical floor.

Five minutes later Laura alighted from the elevator. "What's up, Hilda? Dr. Jeremiah awake?"

The short, ample nurse in her late fifties raised one lightly penciled brow. "So that's his name, eh? No, but Tom Watson was asking for you."

Laura took the chart Hilda handed her and walked swiftly through the door next to the nurses' station. Tom Watson lay in the bed nearest the door, his eyes wide and alert. When he saw the young doctor, he grinned broadly, softening his homely features into pleasant contours beneath his bandaged head.

"How are you feeling, Tom?"

"I'm hurtin' some, Dr. Laura, but thanks be to the Good Lord and you I can feel something, even if it is a little pain. That was a close call and I just wanted to thank you."

"You're right Tom—it was the Good Lord. Physicians can operate and medicate, but the miracle of healing is still in His hands. You can thank Him that you'll be almost as good as new in a few months if you're faithful to your therapy."

"Aye, that I'll be. Jenny and the kids—they'll be needing me. I don't know what I'll do until then."

"We'll figure out something, Tom. You just worry about getting well."

"Anyhow, thanks, Doctor."

Laura took Tom's hand and squeezed it, smiling. "That was my pleasure. I'll check in on you later. I have another patient in the next room, so I'll be here all night if you need me."

Tom's lopsided grin peeped from beneath the heavy bandages. "That's comforting to know, Doctor."

Laura said a quick goodbye and rushed down the hall to the Jeremiah room. She pushed open the door, only to find the scene much as it was when she'd left it, except now only one nurse, lovely and young Gretchen Evans, sat at the temporary station, poring over charts.

The blond, green-eyed girl looked up when Laura entered and smiled. "Dr. Laura, I was just about to page you. His condition is stable, but he's been stirring some and mumbling. Shall I take his blood pressure for you?"

Laura returned the young nurse's smile, shaking her head. She liked Gretchen. The daughter of a miner, she had grown up in Wales and been educated in England, then continued her specialized training in America by taking some graduate courses in Kentucky. Her clipped British accent mingled with the slow Southern cadence spoken in the hospital, creating a strangely pleasing mixture of sounds.

"No, thank you. I will. Suppose you go on to supper. Stop on your way out and tell Hilda you're leaving."

Gretchen looked at her watch and nodded. "See you at half past the hour unless I hear from you before then."

Laura picked up the patient's chart and walked toward the bed, her crepe-soled shoes making whispering sounds on the hard shiny floor. When she reached the bedside, she unbuttoned her jacket and took a stethoscope and a small flashlight from her skirt pocket.

Pausing for a moment, she studied the patient. His color was good; his breathing appeared normal; but his creased brow and the hard set of his mouth indicated that either his dreams were unpleasant or he was experiencing some pain.

She leaned closer. He moaned slightly and the frown deepened as his dark-brown eyes opened to stare blankly into hers.

Laura drew back at the intensity in them, catching her breath in an inaudible gasp; yet she seemed powerless to take her eyes from his. In that unguarded moment before full consciousness arrived, his eyes revealed pure, agonizing heartbreak while at the same time blazing with a fire and vitality that sent shock waves to Laura's innermost being.

She remained close to him, mesmerized by what she saw, yet feeling like an intruder as he grappled to return to consciousness. For a moment she had gazed into the very soul of this man and, unknown to him, witnessed some deep, unidentified longing that tormented him. It both awed and fascinated her.

So entranced by what she saw, she failed to notice one muscular arm move from beneath the sheet. Suddenly, with lightning speed and inconceivable strength, it encircled her neck while his other hand grasped a handful of her hair. He pulled her face to his.

"Mona, Mona. Why? Why?" he groaned as his lips claimed hers.

Too stunned to recoil and too afraid of injuring him by forceful resistance, Laura closed her eyes and waited, locked motionless in the man's embrace, waiting for the inevitable. She knew that soon the adrenaline would expend itself and he would slip limply from his semiconscious state back into oblivion, where he would have no painful recall of the past few moments.

Not so for Laura. Her heart thumped wildly and her inner ears reverberated with the name Mona. Who was she? The source of his agony, perhaps. She knew the answer. His kiss had told her. It contained no tenderness, only a commanding possessiveness. But what about Darlene?

He released her lips and his eyes closed. When Laura turned her head slightly, his arm locked like a vice around her neck and his fingers pulled her long thick hair.

Pushing against the bed with her hands, she maneuvered her body gently, straining to take some of her weight off him, hoping the gentle resistance would free her without injury to him, but his grip only tightened.

She groped for the emergency light and it fell with a clatter to the hard floor. Rising anxiety pumped Laura's heart even more wildly; she was trapped.

She considered her alternatives. She could ring for Hilda, but by the time help arrived Laura might be free. Anyway, she'd just as soon the affable but talkative nurse didn't find her in this situation. It would be the sole topic of hospital conversation by morning and for weeks to come.

She muffled a gasp. Her momentary position was not only embarrassing but painful. If he didn't relax his hold soon she would be forced to call for assistance. The door opened quietly behind her and she heard soft footsteps in the room. Laura whispered, "Hilda? I need some assistance."

Relief flooded Laura when she heard Gretchen's clipped British tones rather than Hilda's slow mountain drawl, as the nurse inquired, "Dr. Laura?" God did cover the foolish mistakes of His children!

"Yes, Gretchen. Hurry!" she said in a voice little more than a murmur but urgent none-the-less. Even now, the patient's welfare still remained uppermost in her mind.

The petite blond nurse sprinted around the bed screen. Her eyes widened with astonishment as she took in the doctor locked in her patient's embrace.

"Careful, now. Don't hurt him. Get my hair untangled first. Then maybe he'll release his hold on my neck voluntarily. If not, we'll have to use force, but you'll have to be very careful or we could injure him."

Gretchen nodded, comprehending instantly, and set to work releasing the long, blond locks from the patient's clasp. Just as the last strand swung free, Laura felt Brad's grip on her neck relax, and knew that his surge of energy had abated at last.

The nurse worked quickly and efficiently to disentangle her from the strong arm—a fairly simple task once he had relinquished his hold. Laura glanced at her watch. What had seemed to last a lifetime had in reality been only four minutes.

Exhausted both emotionally and physically, she dropped into the chair Gretchen pushed over and rubbed her neck, stretching her legs out in front of her. Looking up into the questioning green eyes, she responded wanly, "That is how *not* to handle a delirious patient."

"What happened?"

Gretchen's green eyes took on merry lights as Laura explained in soft but animated tones.

"Was I ever glad to hear your voice, but didn't you eat?"

"The line was too long, and for some strange reason I felt an urgency to come back up here. I'm glad I listened to my conscience."

"I should have known better. I just didn't think," Laura admitted.

Gretchen chuckled melodiously. "Well, you've had a romantic afternoon!" then amended when she observed Laura's threatening look, "I can see how that happened. Pardon me for saying so, but even in his present condition, he is a fascinating man."

Laura responded with a startled, "Why, Gretchen!"

"Well, it's the truth—speaking purely from an unprofessional point of view, that is. He's handsome and mysterious, and from your description has a very commanding presence, even when he's delirious. If he'd looked at anyone like that, it would have caught her off guard. It happened to me once at a hospital in Wales. There had been an accident in one of the mines and an injured miner pinioned me when he came out from under the anesthesia. It took two doctors to loose me and I was the hospital joke for a month.''

Laura looked at Gretchen gratefully. Her green eyes had lost their merriment and gazed steadily into Laura's blue ones; an unspoken understanding passed between the two women as a deepening bond of friendship and understanding was established. There would be no idle chatter about this event; only the essentials would be noted on the patient's chart.

''Why don't you go get a cup of tea before the dining hall closes, and pick me up a sandwich and bring it back. That little show will have exhausted him, so he'll sleep at least for another hour. I can handle things here until then. If there is any change, I'll ring you immediately,'' Gretchen gently suggested.

''The way I was able to ring you?''

Merry lights once again danced in the nurse's expressive eyes. ''Well, he's not my type. Now, if he were more like Dr. Mark—''

''Gretchen!'' Laura reprimanded.

The nurse thrust up one hand defensively. ''Just couldn't resist that, Boss. But you really don't have to worry—my hair's not as long!'' she finished with an impish grin and a toss of her short, red-gold curls.

Laura grimaced, then chuckled. "Suppose I pick you up a sandwich and then take a walk around the grounds. Perhaps some fresh air will liven me up a bit."

"Dr. Laura, I don't think you were careless. It was just a freak happening. Who would ever have thought you looked like someone he knew and that he'd be that strong?"

"I don't know if he really saw me or not. I should have been more alert. I only hope that he didn't harm his recovery any."

"It didn't harm that coal miner. The only thing that hurt was my pride."

"I can identify with that, but must admit if the only casualty is my pride, I'll be thankful and relieved," Laura said, nodding slightly. Then, with a thoughtful look, she added, "Wonder who this Mona is. She must be something to affect a man that much."

The brisk walk to the edge of the gorge completely rejuvenated Laura, and she put the strange occurrence into proper perspective, which relieved some of her chagrin. In evaluating the experience, she had to admit that her emotional response to the patient had kept her from being as alert as she should have been, but even if she had seen him move his arm, she'd never have expected him to grab her. No, the result would have been the same.

She traced her lips and once again a soft blush washed her face as she remembered the intensity of his kiss. Then she shuddered as the raw pain in his eyes swam before hers.

A wry smile curled one side of her mouth. She was thankful he wouldn't remember the incident, but she knew it would continue to haunt the chambers of her mind. One couldn't see into the very soul of a person and dismiss it casually.

Her smile brightened when she recalled that Gretchen rather than Hilda had arrived on the scene. At least publicly her pride would be spared. The clinic was fortunate to have Gretchen working there. Laura knew little about Gretchen's nonprofessional life, but from her own experience she was aware that the surrounding area offered little excitement for a young person. Beyond a movie and church socials, life was pretty staid. So, she wondered, what was life like for Gretchen? What kept her buried in a small hospital in Kentucky? Did she have any friends and was there a special someone Laura had yet to meet? As Laura puzzled these questions, she felt a nagging sense of regret that she had not taken the time to get to know Gretchen better.

She glanced at her watch. Better get back inside those walls. Maybe she and Gretchen could take in a movie or something together sometimes. It'd be nice to have time for a friend—other than Mark, that is. Now, what was it Gretchen had said about Mark? Hmm.

Hilda and Gretchen sat on the tall stools behind the stainless-steel counter in the room, talking in excited but low tones. The screen had been moved from around Dr. Jeremiah's bed and he was in full view of the two nurses.

The older nurse looked at Laura and smiled. For a moment the doctor's heart sank. Here it comes, she thought, the teasing.

"Well, Dr. Laura, we were just discussing how we could find you. Then we opened the blinds and there you were, enjoying the sunset from the edge of the gorge. I told Gretchen you sure were younger and more energetic than me," Hilda observed amiably.

"I thought I was the only one who loved that view. I try to take my supper break just in time to work in a peek," Gretchen chimed in.

"I rather spoiled that for you tonight, but I'm glad you rearranged your schedule. Your assistance proved invaluable," Laura responded.

Hilda quirked an eyebrow. "Did I miss something?"

Gretchen countered with a smooth chuckle. "You, Hilda? Do you ever miss anything? The patient was a little restless coming out from under the anesthesia and it took both Dr. Laura and me to calm him. But it was all in a day's work."

Laura smiled appreciatively. "And how is the patient?"

"He's stirring some. Believe he's about to wake up. Hope he's more cognizant this time."

Laura turned from the nurses and went to stand at the foot of the bed, then hesitantly proceeded halfway around the bed to stand safely away from the strong arms resting quietly on top of the sheet.

The dark-brown eyes opened slowly, but this time they widened, a puzzled expression wrinkling the broad smooth brow.

Laura smiled and answered the unasked question. "Good afternoon, Dr. Jeremiah. I'm Dr. Laura McBride and you are at the Appalachian Clinic in Broadbank, Kentucky. We need to get some information from you if you feel like talking."

The man made no verbal response; his eyes merely darkened and his frown deepened. Laura could see his agitation growing and she continued in a soothing voice, "You have been in an accident, but you're doing fine and should completely recover. Are there any people you would like for us to notify to relieve their mind as to your whereabouts?"

"What kind of accident?" he asked tersely.

"Your airplane. You encountered some bad weather and engine trouble. You crashed on the side of the mountain but were able to crawl to safety. We assumed there was no one with you. Was there?"

He waited a long moment before he answered softly, looking straight into Laura's eyes, his filled with anguish, "I don't know."

"You don't know?"

"I mean, I can't remember," he answered impatiently.

Laura smiled reassuringly. "I see. Don't be alarmed. Sometimes it takes several hours after an accident for people to get their bearings. You'll be fine as you become more alert."

"I am alert. Don't you understand? I don't remember anything. Not just about the accident but anything, not who I am, where I was going!" Something akin to panic glittered in his eyes.

"Transitory amnesia is not uncommon with an accident patient, especially one who has taken a blow to the head.''

He lifted his hand and touched the bandage on his forehead. ''Blow to the head?''

''Yes.'' Laura nodded. ''And surgery.''

''You operated on me?''

''No, my father, Dr. David McBride, performed emergency surgery last night to relieve intercranial pressure. So you see, it could even take several days for your memory to return to normal. The most important thing for you to realize is that you must remain calm and patient.''

''Easy enough for you to say,'' he growled. ''Where is this McBride?''

''He's not available this evening.''

''And what if I have an emergency?''

''I'm on duty and can assure you that I am qualified to administer aid and answer your questions,'' she replied patiently and calmly, while the blood rushed to her face.

''I'm not satisfied with your answers. I need someone to help me remember, not tell me to be patient.'' His voice rose in agitation.

''Dr. Jeremiah, I understand your concern. You are still sedated and suffering severe trauma. In most cases memory returns right away. If you should need further assistance, we do have a fully staffed hospital to help you.''

''I thought you said clinic,'' he stated, his eyes still wary.

''It used to be a clinic. The name is still the same,

but it is now a fully acredited hospital, equipped to handle any type of accident case.''

"What did you call me?"

"Dr. Jeremiah." Laura smiled, anticipating the next question.

"How did you know my name? Is this my home?"

"No, of course not. You are Dr. Michael Bradford Jeremiah of Medical Surgeons and Associates in Louisville, Kentucky."

"You found some identification, I take it."

"Actually, no. Strangely enough, I met you just this past weekend in Louisville. I was visiting with Darlene Coleman—"

"Darlene—who is Darlene?"

Laura's heart sank. What if his amnesia wasn't the lingering effect of coma and anesthesia? What if he truly couldn't remember who he was? How could anyone cope with that?

"Darlene was my old med school suite mate and you are..." Laura wasn't sure how to describe their relationship. At this point, the least said the better, she decided. "An acquaintance of hers. In fact, you are in the same medical practice together."

"What kind of joke do you think this is? I'd remember if I were a physician. I've never heard of any Darlene Coleman. And I've never seen you before, either."

"I can assure you that I would not play such a cruel joke on anyone. But then, it isn't anything to be alarmed about. Your memory should return soon. Meanwhile, I need to take your blood pressure and give you an injection to help you rest."

"Rest? I don't want to rest."

"Believe me, the best way to recover your memory is to remain calm and let your body heal."

Laura's tone of quiet authority seemed to reach him and his agitation eased. He held out his arm to her and she slipped the cuff onto his muscular arm. He turned toward the window and away from her, as if to ignore her would remove his problem.

A sudden compassion for him flooded Laura and she tried once more to soothe him. "I'm not taking your condition lightly. I can only imagine how frustrated you must be now, but I've seen this condition many times and I know it isn't permanent."

"Perhaps not, young lady—"

"'Dr. McBride,'" Laura's corrected, her pride responding to his condescending tone.

"Yes, well, if you think your shot will help, please proceed. And when I awake—"

"Probably another physician will see you and perhaps we'll have more information," Laura countered.

"And my memory?"

"I can't promise you how soon it will return, but it will. I can assure you that you will receive the very best medical attention available and every effort will be made to assist you in recovering your memory."

Even as Laura talked she examined his eyes for signs of serious brain injury. Finding none, and his blood pressure only slightly elevated, she painlessly and efficiently administered a heavy sedative.

Without warning a charming one-sided grin replaced the fierce expression on her patient's face. In a half-apologetic tone he drawled, "I guess I must like being in control, but if I have to be dependent I couldn't have found a lovelier companion.''

Laura's smiling response corrected stubbornly, '' 'Doctor,'—and thank you, I think.'' As a flash of the old Dr. Jeremiah appeared, the memory of their first meeting filled her mind.

"Now, you relax. The medication will take effect in just a few minutes. If you need me I'll be in this room or the next until I go off duty.''

"Thank you, Doctor. I shall rest easier with that knowledge, I'm sure,'' he responded, closing his eyes before Laura could tell whether his remark was serious or cynical.

"I fully expect you will sleep until morning, at which time Dr. David McBride or Dr. Mark Harrod will attend you. They are superb physicians, trained in treating trauma victims,'' Laura assured.

He nodded silently, as if the brief conversation had once again expended his energy. Then, as he closed his eyes, he remarked docilely, "Thank you again, Doctor. I'm sure I'll be better in the morning.''

This time there was no doubt in Laura's mind that he meant what he said. And she was grateful he had regained hope. Now she prayed that when he did awake, so would his memory. Until then, she faced a long night.

Chapter Five

By the time Darlene arrived on Thursday, Brad Jeremiah's physical condition had improved, but his memory had not returned. After concluding he was out of danger, David and Mark had moved him out of intensive care and into their most luxurious room, one whose window looked out on Thunderbolt Gorge and the mountains beyond. They had hoped it would lift his spirits, but the move was to no avail.

Jeremiah alternated between anxiety and depression. Proving a difficult patient, he demanded answers beyond the staff's ability to respond and extra attention from the overworked personnel of the small hospital.

It was with a sigh of relief mixed with trepidation that Laura spied Darlene's black convertible wheel into the hospital parking lot. At Laura's insistence her friend had rearranged her appointments and arrived a day earlier than expected.

Maybe seeing her would spark Brad Jeremiah's memory and put him on the road to recovery. But what if it didn't? Laura didn't even want to consider that possibility. Darlene was her only link to Dr. Jeremiah's past. The biggest problem that Laura faced now was telling her friend the nature of Brad's illness.

She had delayed informing her, hoping his amnesia was only transient and would return before her friend's arrival. It hadn't, and now she faced the unpleasant duty of being the bearer of ill tidings. She only hoped that her former suite mate would not be angry with her for withholding the details of Brad's condition.

Darlene breezed through the door, spilling the sweet, provocative fragrance of orange blossoms in her wake, her white suit immaculate. Her eyes were bright with anxiety as Laura met her in the lobby.

"What is his condition now? I've moved heaven and earth to be here. Is he in danger? I thought you said his injuries weren't serious—"

"No, Darlene. I said his injuries weren't life threatening. The first night was touch-and-go, but after he pulled through that, we were sure he would recover."

"Then what urgency dictated that I come sooner than planned?" Darlene demanded.

"Brad has amnesia."

"Is that all?" Relief softened her voice.

"He's an emotional wreck, alternating between extreme anxiety and depression." Laura rushed on to explain, refusing to apologize for involving her reluctant friend.

"Brad Jeremiah an emotional wreck? I can't imagine that," Darlene disputed.

"Well, he is. Put yourself in his place for a moment. Must be an unnerving experience," Laura noted, mystified at Darlene's cold response.

"Perhaps for someone who isn't a doctor. But a physician should know it's only a temporary condition."

"But he doesn't know he is a physician. He has amnesia," Laura said, her patience wearing thin.

"He had a blow to the head, I take it," Darlene stated in a tone that trivialized the whole incident.

"Quite a severe blow," Laura added.

"You know as well as I, temporary amnesia is not uncommon when one has had trauma of the type Brad experienced. I'm surprised that you of all people are alarmed, Laura," Darlene commented, somewhat condescendingly.

Laura pushed back a short retort, reminding herself that her friend's reaction closely resembled denial. "Exactly, but since it is having a devastating effect on Dr. Jeremiah, we had hoped that when he saw you, it would jolt his memory."

Darlene nodded, all physician now. "I understand. Well, let's get it over with. I've got to get back to my practice as soon as possible. It will be on my shoulders to keep our business going until Brad returns. I had no idea we had a potential problem."

"If his memory doesn't return, you won't have a partner," Laura stubbornly reminded her.

"More to the point, if his memory doesn't return soon we won't have a practice. Much of our business is because of Brad. He has a way with women." Darlene laughed.

"Not that I've noticed," Laura murmured, remembering the past few days and her difficult and demanding patient.

"Well, it's obvious he's not himself. I'm sure when I talk to him, he'll be able to find his way back."

"I fervently hope so," Laura answered tensely, then took Darlene up to Brad's room.

Dr. Brad Jeremiah stared morosely out the large window in his room, as if he hadn't heard the two women enter.

Darlene's high heels clicked a staccato rhythm as she resolutely approached his bed. She crooned, "Darling, how are you?"

When he finally turned toward them, acknowledging their presence, she bent toward him as if to kiss him.

He jerked away from her, demanding of Laura, "Who is this woman?"

"Who indeed but your fiancée and business partner, dear," Darlene answered sharply.

Brad Jeremiah twisted to the far side of the bed, and his brown eyes, cold and calculating, took Darlene in from head to foot. "Surely I'd remember a detail like that."

"Of course you're going to remember. It's just a matter of time."

"That's what these doctors around here tell me. But it hasn't happened, and furthermore, I don't have a clue who you are." Then he paused, a frown wrinkling his brow, before he asked, "Are you Mona?"

Darlene's face whitened and she asked through tight lips, "What does Mona have to do with this?"

Jeremiah shrugged. "Are you Mona?"

"No, I'm not Mona." Darlene looked at a mystified Laura. "I thought you said he can't remember anything."

"He can't."

"What about Mona?"

"Ladies, would you quit discussing me as if I were not present. The little doctor here told me I mentioned Mona before I came out of my coma. That's all. I take it you're not Mona?"

"No, I am not Mona. I am Darlene."

"Well, who is Mona?"

"Mona is Dr. Gilbreth's daughter."

"And who is Dr. Gilbreth?"

"The physician who started the practice we are in."

"Well, what's Mona got to do with anything?"

"I can't imagine," Darlene responded, her eyes dull.

Laura looked from one to the other in amazement, her curiosity piqued. Darlene was lying. But why?

"Perhaps you could tell him a little about his life in Louisville. Show him some pictures if you have any. Anything familiar that might be a key," Laura suggested as she backed out of the room, eager to escape and leave the field to Darlene.

Two hours later the sound of Darlene's high heels against the tile floor resounded down the quiet corridor, but this time the footsteps came slowly, less confidently. Laura saw in the set of Darlene's shoulders that her mission had proved unsuccessful.

"Not much progress?" she asked quietly.

"None at all," Darlene responded glumly.

"What you need is a cup of tea. Let's go over to the house and we can talk."

"I really shouldn't."

"Nonsense. By the time you get back home, the work day would be over. I was sort of hoping you'd be able to stay through the weekend—"

"Absolutely out of the question," Darlene interrupted.

"Really?"

"Yes, really. I shall have to leave Dr. Jeremiah in your capable hands, while I try to hold on to our practice. You understand?"

"Not exactly." A frown wrinkled Laura's smooth brow, her eyes questioning. "You have time for tea, Darlene. We need to talk."

Seeing the determination in her friend's eyes, Darlene reluctantly agreed and turned toward the door and her car.

A warm May breeze caressed Laura's face and a hint of sweet shrub teased her nostrils. She leaned against the brick wall of the farmhouse patio and stared down into the green valley below her that was just awakening to spring. For a moment, she forgot her friend behind her and the anxieties of the moment. She took a deep breath and relished the crisp clean air.

Today, as in the past, this spot proved a respite for her. Although it had no power to resolve her problems, from this vista she often gained a new perspective. Perhaps Darlene, too, would find some solace here, away from the bustling city and its pressures. She sensed in Darlene a troubled spirit that went beyond her immediate problem with Brad and his recovery. Perhaps if her friend could relax and shed her sleek facade, Laura could reach her, help her with whatever troubled her. At least she could lend a listening ear. Sometimes that was all a person needed.

Darlene stepped through the broad French doors and joined Laura on the patio. "What a view. I can see why you love it here."

Laura smiled, pleased that her friend approved. "I love it for several reasons, not the least of which is that my roots are here."

"Something neither Brad nor I have a sense of," Darlene remarked, a yearning touching her dark eyes.

"I guess it's something that can be easily taken for granted," Laura said.

"Unless you don't have it. There was a time when I envied you that."

"Why?"

"Because you had a sense of family, of belonging, that I didn't have."

"But you have family. A quite successful one, if I remember."

"Success in business does not necessarily mean successful family relationships. There never seemed to be time for both."

"You don't have to make the same mistakes."

"Aren't we inclined to follow in our family's footsteps? As you reminded me in Louisville, we get our value system from our families."

"Is that what you're doing?" Laura probed.

"Let's just say that I've come to appreciate their values. In the final analysis career and financial achievements are the tangible measurements of success. And I do want to be a success."

"What is your definition of success?" Laura asked.

"Wealth, prestige and a suitable marriage."

"In that order?" Laura asked, her voice as soft as the whispering breeze that surrounded them.

Darlene bit her lip. "Yes, I think so."

"How does Brad Jeremiah fit in?"

"I am extremely fortunate that the man with whom I fell in love fits perfectly with my career choices." Darlene turned from Laura to gaze out into the distant valley.

"How convenient," Laura drawled.

Darlene chuckled mirthlessly. "Not too convenient at the present. This accident throws a big kink into our plans. That is, unless Brad recovers pronto."

"Thoughtless of him."

"You might say that. If he had stayed out of that plane, this wouldn't have happened." Bitterness tinged Darlene's practiced dulcimer tones.

"Do you have any idea where he was going?"

"How should I know? I was making my rounds— and his, I might add. The only thing he told me was that he had some pressing business out of town and wanted me to cover for him a couple of days. We would have to check his flight plan to see where he was going."

"Must have been something really pressing, considering the weather. Surely he checked the weather advisories before he left," Laura suggested.

Darlene dropped her eyes, unwilling to meet Laura's questioning gaze. "Who knows? It's unimportant now anyway. What matters is his speedy recovery, which I'm going to leave in your capable hands. I just cannot abandon our practice to nurse him. If I let anything happen to it, he would never forgive me."

"Sounds as if you share similar goals."

"Couldn't be more compatible. We need each other, and beyond that, I love him and intend to have him, one way or another."

"Was there any doubt of that?"

Darlene's triumphant smile dazzled. "No. And quite a change from that little mousey wallflower you roomed with, eh?" The soft yearning had exited, leaving only a determined light in eyes that seemed brittle and cold.

Laura shivered as she nodded thoughtfully. "Quite a change indeed."

A sense of foreboding weighed Laura down after Darlene's departure. Her former suite mate's visit did nothing to alleviate the hospital's problems with their ill-humored patient; if anything, he became more uncooperative and demanding. The "helpful" conversation she had envisioned with her friend had for all practical purposes failed. Now Laura was left with a heavier burden of responsibility for Brad's recovery.

Laura opened her blinds to a sky whose pink-and-golden fingers of dawn announced a new day. Taking a deep breath, she lifted her hands heavenward and stretched. Somehow today Dr. Brad Jeremiah would make progress; she felt it in her bones.

Gretchen met Laura at the nurses' station, consternation written on her face. "Dr. Laura, Dr. Jeremiah is in rare form. So far he's refused his medication, sent his tray back three times because it was not to his liking and is demanding a transfer to another wing. He doesn't think his mattress is comfortable and he's tired of the view."

Laura smiled and took his chart. "Is that right, Gretchen? Is my father or Mark here?"

"No. They had an all-day conference to attend. You're in charge."

"Well, fine. I think it's time we give Dr. Brad Jeremiah some cooperation."

"He has the nicest room in the hospital and the kitchen has gone to all kinds of trouble to accommodate his preferences. There's just no pleasing him." Gretchen, usually unflappable, seemed close to tears.

"I'll deal with him," Laura assured her as she entered Jeremiah's room.

"Ms. McBride," Jeremiah snarled.

"That's 'Dr.' McBride, Dr. Jeremiah," Laura quietly corrected.

"Oh, pardon me," he crooned. "Since I've seen you do little more than a nurse does, I keep forgetting you're a real doctor."

A flush mounted Laura's face, but she responded firmly without emotion, "It may surprise you, Dr. Jeremiah, but I don't need you to verify my duties to qualify my position here. I am a fully certified physician, and furthermore, I am the one on duty and in charge.''

Brad Jeremiah's eyes widened at the note of authority in her voice. "If you're really in charge maybe you can get something done for me. This inefficient staff is nothing but a joke. If I were the doctor in charge, I would make a lot of changes around here.''

"How can I help you?" Laura inquired briskly.

"This room is deplorable. The bed is uncomfortable and the food is not edible. As for the room, I want another. This one just won't do.''

Laura pretended to study his chart carefully. "And your medication. I see you refused it.''

"It's that nurse. She no more knows how to give a shot than someone off the street.''

"So you want another room and another nurse, do you?''

"Absolutely.''

"Dr. Jeremiah, since you are so unhappy in these surroundings, I suggest you transfer to Medical Center in Louisville. Darlene would be nearby, which should prove comforting to you.''

He jerked up his head, a touch of fear in his eyes. "I'm not going to another hospital. You know I'm too ill to travel.''

Laura smiled cheerfully. "I know nothing of the sort. Your leg is mending quite well, and your memory might return more quickly if you were back in familiar surroundings.''

"I told you I'm not going. Anyway, it wouldn't be familiar to me."

"I see. What do you suggest, then?"

"I'm not suggesting anything. I'm telling you to get me another room and another nurse."

"If that's what it takes to make you happy, Dr. Jeremiah, I think we can handle that without a problem," Laura said.

"It's about time you listened to me," Jeremiah growled to Laura's back as she exited.

"Gretchen, where is Bertha scheduled to work this week?"

Gretchen's eyes widened. "Big Bertha?"

"The very same."

"She's on B wing downstairs."

"That's where that oversize storage room is located. Perfect," Laura mumbled, nodding thoughtfully. "He wants a change of venue. Let's accommodate him. Have the orderlies clean out the supply room and put a bed in there."

"For—for?" Gretchen stammered.

Laura nodded. "You guessed it."

"But, but, but, there's no closet, no bathroom," Gretchen argued.

"As I remember, there is a lavatory where he can brush his teeth. A walk down the hall will be good therapy for him, since so far he has refused to cooperate with the therapist. He hasn't any clothes, so he won't need a closet. It's just perfect," Laura announced, beaming as she closed his chart.

"And Big Bertha, too?" Gretchen questioned.

"As I said, Gretchen, it sounds perfect." Laura's

smile broadened as the vision of Bertha Love invaded her mind. Of sturdy mountain stock, Bertha had reached her physical potential and then some. She was a tall broad woman, whose brusque and no-nonsense manner intimidated all except those who knew her imposing exterior covered a heart of gold. But for Laura's purposes Dr. Jeremiah would discover that secret only after his cooperation was well in hand.

"He will be incensed." Gretchen held her eyes for a long searching moment.

"You're convinced, are you?" she asked in her delightful British, suddenly friend more than employee.

Laura nodded resolutely. Then Gretchen giggled.

"What is the meaning of this?" Brad Jeremiah demanded when Laura made her afternoon rounds.

"Meaning of what, Dr. Jeremiah?" Laura asked innocently as she listened to his pounding heart.

"This hole in the hall your staff calls a room."

"You mean your new accommodations?"

"This arrangement you call 'accommodations'?" he all but shouted.

"You wanted a new room and a new bed—this is all that is available."

He crossed his arms and stared at her, his dark eyes blazing. "Then I'll go back to where I was."

"Sorry, but that room is no longer available."

"Then make it available."

"The occupant of that room needs assistance far more than you and, I might add, cooperates with us.

It will be quite impossible for you to have any other room but this one."

"And another thing, that pretty little nurse hasn't even been in here to check my vital signs. Do you call that any way to take care of a patient?"

"She's not your nurse anymore. Anyhow, I thought she displeased you."

"Not necessarily," Jeremiah mumbled into his covers.

"This is not Gretchen's floor."

"Whoever she is, I haven't seen a soul since they moved me into this godforsaken hole."

"He hasn't forsaken you, Dr. Jeremiah. You've blocked Him out with all your ranting, raving and self-pity," Laura observed calmly as she placed her stethoscope in her pocket.

"What? How dare you talk to me like that! You don't know what it's like, not remembering who you are."

"I'm sure it's a terrifying experience, Brad." Laura's tone gentled as she met and held his gaze for a moment.

"Who said I was terrified? I'm angry, not scared," he insisted, dropping his gaze, but not before Laura glimpsed the truth.

"You're scared. The sooner you admit it and start cooperating, the sooner you'll recover."

He looked up again; this time a hint of a smile tugged at his mouth. "Can you promise that I'll recover if I behave, Lady Doctor?"

"I can assure you your cooperation will be the first step toward recovery, but no one can tell you how long the journey will take. However, before you can arrive at any destination, you must begin.''

''And you think I've delayed the process?''

Laura nodded. ''By fighting the truth.''

He quirked a brow toward her, his eyes holding hers. ''The truth?''

''That you're afraid.''

''What am I afraid of?''

''That you may not recover?''

Brad lay back against the pillows and closed his eyes. ''Maybe.''

''That's a beginning.''

''What next?'' He opened his eyes, which were warmer as the hostility drained away.

''How about starting with some cooperation?''

''I've been uncooperative?'' he asked with a mock scowl.

''That's putting it mildly.''

''From now on I'll be putty in your hands. I'll prove it. Call one of your pretty li'l nurses and I'll let her medicate to her heart's desire. I'll even roll up my sleeve for one of those pesky shots you love to order for me.''

''Well, here she comes now, Dr. Jeremiah. Roll up your sleeve,'' Laura said just as Bertha lumbered into the room.

''So you're my new patient,'' Bertha boomed, her gravely voice matching her two hundred-pound frame.

''You're my nurse?'' He cast Laura a look of desperation.

"Yep. I get all the special cases," the nurse replied, a satisfied look on her face.

"Special?"

"Well... Maybe challenging might be more nearly the truth."

"You heard I was a challenge?"

"More or less," she stated, as Laura watched the exchange scarcely able to contain her amusement.

"You have received the wrong information. I'm as gentle as a lamb. See? I'm all ready for you."

"That's good. I hate to have to use my powers of persuasion."

"So would I," Jeremiah agreed as he held out his arm for his shot.

"I'll be back in with your dinner shortly. I guess you're hungry, eh?"

"I could eat a horse."

"We don't eat horses here—we ride them. But I'll expect you to eat whatever I bring you. You're looking kinda peaked."

"Yes, ma'am. You bring it and I'll eat it," he remarked to her sturdy departing back.

"What have you done to me?" Brad demanded of Laura after Bertha left.

"I think Bertha explained it well. You insisted on special care. Therefore, that's what you get. Bertha is assigned to the most special cases." Laura raised her eyebrows questioningly.

"Thanks." Brad sighed.

"My pleasure," Laura responded.

"I can see you're enjoying yourself immensely."

"As I told you earlier, Dr. Jeremiah, we will be glad to transfer you to the city," Laura reminded him.

"No, thank you. I'll stay here."

"Big Bertha and all?"

"Yes."

"Small room, bad food and intimidating nurse can't persuade you to leave?"

"Other than my bad disposition, why do you want to be rid of me?"

"Your disposition is enough reason, but the main one is I want you to get well. I thought familiar surroundings might speed your recovery. Why don't you want to go?"

"Fear."

"Oh?"

"People will know me and I won't know them. They will know things about me that I don't know about myself. That would bother me. I'd rather stay here, where we're more or less on even ground. You know I was a physician and where I came from. You met me once. Other than that we'll learn who I am together, until my memory kicks in. I'm more comfortable with that avenue."

"Are you afraid to find out who you are, Brad?"

"Perhaps. Or maybe what I was. Isn't amnesia sometimes a psychological phenomenon when a person wants to block out unpleasant reality?"

"That's correct. Is some of your medical knowledge returning, or did you look up the word somehow?"

"Somehow it was a fact just sitting there in my

mind, like what two plus two is or my ability to speak and communicate.''

"Even so, that's very encouraging.''

"Perhaps it's because I've quit fighting.''

"Have you?''

Brad looked up. "Can I go back to my room now and get my same little nurse back?'' he pleaded.

"Liked cute little Gretchen, eh?''

"Yep, but she was also an excellent nurse.''

"She'll be glad to hear you said that since you had her in tears this morning,'' Laura remarked dryly.

"Well, can I?''

"Nothing doing. I told you—another, more needy, patient has that room. Truly, this is all that is available.''

He shuddered. "And Heaven help me if I'm not cooperative!''

Laura laughed. "Brad, in the final analysis, only Heaven can help you.''

Chapter Six

Dr. David McBride strode down the corridor deep in thought, his head down. As he turned into his office, Mark hailed him from his open door, but David never heard him.

"Ginger, page Laura and have her come to my office," he commanded over his shoulder, then entered his office and closed the door. He sank into his chair and leaned back. Then he lifted his feet and placed them on his desk, carefully maneuvering among the stacks of charts there awaiting his attention. Putting his hand across his eyes, he closed them and sighed deeply, fatigue written in every line of his body.

Thus it was that Mark found him. He knocked and entered without waiting for permission. One look at his boss and he pursed his lips. "Things as bad as that?"

"Just frustrating, Mark. Why can't a physician just

doctor? I would like to get back to helping people and forget all this administrative frustration.''

Alarmed at David's distress, Mark reminded him, ''You're just tired. You haven't had a day off in weeks.''

''I never realized I would have to spend so many hours attending to reams of bureaucratic red tape, time I'd rather spend with patients and my research projects.''

''Have you ever considered slowing down, David?''

''You mean dreamed of it? Sure. I dream of having the time to accept some of these invitations to lecture and get the word out about what we are accomplishing here with so little support. I long for time to organize my notes, to get them published.''

''Then grab Cassie and that laptop of hers and be on your way.''

David chuckled, his mind filled with the image of his petite, dark-eyed wife. ''That's a very tempting suggestion, Harrod, but don't you dare say a word about this to Cassie or she will have her bags packed before morning.''

''Cassie knows you can't continue at the pace you're going. We all do, David.''

''Mark, you know I can't go. Who would we get to run things? Not you. You've already told me you wouldn't be interested in the administrative duties of a hospital.''

''Don't you think God will provide someone if He is redirecting your life?''

''I would have to be very sure this was His direction. There was such certainty that He sent me when I came, I never considered He would ever redirect me. Anyway, until we had someone come on board who could handle my job, it's a moot question.''

"What about Laura?"

"She's not ready for that much responsibility," David retorted.

"Don't sell her short, David."

"You think I do that?"

"Sometimes. As her parent, you're inclined to set a different standard for her," Mark said choosing his words carefully.

"I have to require more from her," David argued, his jaw thrust out obstinately.

"Perhaps, but I'm afraid we have been slow to encourage her development. Maybe you still see her as your little girl, instead of the capable woman she is," Mark gently suggested, knowing he was treading on dangerous ground.

"Speaking of Laura," David began, refusing to acknowledge what Mark had said, "she may have added to our problems with this Brad Jeremiah case."

"You think Laura has done something to make matters worse?"

"He was causing so much trouble she moved him from that nice room we had him in."

Mark started chuckling. "You know where she moved him?"

"Yes, and I fail to see anything humorous in the situation." David drew his brows together sternly.

"You can ease your mind, Dr. McBride Sr. When I looked in on him, he was as docile as a lamb. Bertha had him well in hand. Fact is, he ate his entire supper, and the therapist indicated he had done quite well this afternoon.''

''You don't say!''

''And that's not all—''

''You wanted to see me, Dad?'' Laura interrupted from the door.

''Yes, kitten,'' David responded, his mood suddenly lighter.

''What magic did you weave on our prima donna, Dr. Jeremiah, Laura?'' Mark asked, his eyes dancing merrily.

''Nothing that I know of. He just demanded another room and another nurse, so I complied,'' Laura replied, a feigned innocence widening her eyes.

''Well, you did something to tame that tiger.''

''I only gave the man what he asked for,'' she denied with a smile.

''More than that, I'd say. I was just in his room. Did you know David and I are no longer on the case? He has requested you,'' Mark announced with a broad smile.

David's feet came off the desk and he bolted upright. ''Say what?''

''You heard me. Our difficult patient has requested Dr. Laura McBride as his exclusive physician. Much to my delight, I might add. I spent more time with him than all my other patients.''

''Are you sure, Mark?'' Laura asked, puzzlement wrinkling her forehead.

''Just came from his 'room' and heard it from his own lips, and Bertha had written the request on his chart. So what do you think of those apples, little Ms. Miracle Worker?" Mark teased.

"I'm overwhelmed." Laura lifted her hands, a bewildered expression on her face.

"What did you do, Laura? It seems everyone has found this amusing but me," David remarked gently, this time interest rather than anxiety sparking his intense blue eyes.

"I had a good long talk with him and seemed to get through that hostility. I didn't know how long it would last, but he promised to cooperate. I couldn't be more encouraged."

"Nor I." David sighed, leaned back in his chair and looked up at the ceiling as if a thousand miles away. Then he murmured, "Mark, I think that I'll go home to my wife before dark for a change."

"And I'm going to take our heroine out on the town, if I have her dad's permission," Mark responded.

"By all means. She deserves to celebrate," her dad said approvingly, relief easing the heaviness in his eyes.

Thunderheads banked the western sky as Laura met Mark at the door. She glanced warily at them, remembering the aftermath of the last storm that had pelted their area, and shuddered. Tonight she would put that aside. She looked forward to a lighthearted evening with Mark.

He looked handsome in his navy blazer and she remembered Gretchen's comments. Was he aware of the young nurse's feelings for him? Laura turned toward him in the car, observing his clean-cut profile, his strong, adept hands as they lightly grasped the steering wheel, and finally his broad shoulders atop a lanky frame. How many other women in this small community had a secret crush on him? Trying to see him as other women must, she had to admit Dr. Mark not only had a winsome personality but was also extremely handsome. What woman could fail to be attracted to him?

Mark paused before turning onto the road and grinned his one-sided grin. "I hope I passed inspection, ma'am."

She blushed. Did nothing escape his notice?

Suddenly, the dark brooding eyes of Brad Jeremiah came between her and Mark's merry brown ones. Unbidden thoughts of an evening with her difficult patient filled her mind and she wondered what it would be like. For some reason her heart fluttered.

Resolutely, she put the mysterious city doctor from her mind, reached over to Mark and placed her hand on his arm. Tonight belonged to Mark, and she determined they would have a memorable evening. She felt his muscle tense beneath her light touch as he turned to look at her, his heart in his eyes.

Three weeks following the plane crash, Brad Jeremiah hobbled down the corridor on two crutches to meet Laura at the hospital door. He wore a bright plaid flannel robe that Laura had scrounged from her grandfather and Laura suppressed a smile. With his thick curls tousled and his clothes rumpled, he looked more boy than man. His eyes had a mischievous grin that completely disarmed her.

"From where did this good humor originate, Dr. Jeremiah?" she asked, a broad smile parting her face. Although he had cooperated with them lately, his moods had still ranged from total despair to lethargic complacency.

"The therapist said I was progressing so rapidly I should be able to throw away these crutches shortly," he explained, his eyes dancing with enthusiasm. "And I had a flash of memory today, too."

Laura halted, her eyes reflecting his excitement. "What did you remember?"

"It was more a flash, like an elusive image that came and went. It seemed to be an apartment with a view of some river from a large window several stories high."

"That's your apartment, Brad. I remember that very window with the terrific view."

"I thought it might be, but I was afraid to hope."

"With the therapist's good news, I think you're ready to return home. We could transfer all your records and Darlene would be more than happy to look after you." Relief mingled with an indefinable emotion in her eyes.

At the mention of Darlene's name, a frown dimmed the light in his eyes. "I'm not ready for that."

"Why not? You should recover your memory more quickly in familiar surroundings, and Darlene would devote herself to that project."

His mouth twisted in a cynical smile. "I'm sure of that. Her visits have been just short of browbeating.

She cajoles me to remember things that I can't. In fact, I don't want to see her again until I recover. As my doctor, tell her not to visit again.''

Laura turned to walk away. ''Oh, no, you'll have to tell her. I'm not going to get involved.''

''She left her number. I'll call and tell her not to come Friday,'' he said, hobbling down the hall and speaking to the back of Laura's head.

Laura paused and turned toward Brad, her face almost colliding with his chest. She looked up thoughtfully and asked, ''Is Darlene the reason you don't want to go back to your apartment?''

''Not the only reason. I don't think it would be good to change doctors in midstream.''

''Brad, you've done nothing but complain about our slow progress. Perhaps in Louisville you could see someone more specifically trained in amnesia cases!'' Laura exclaimed, hands on hips in exasperation.

''You used every ploy to persuade me, from Big Bertha to a postage stamp room,'' he reminded her.

Laura flushed. ''My only motive has been your progress.''

''And I've progressed.''

''You've progressed,'' Laura agreed, ''to the point of leaving the hospital. We need this room, so you can't stay here beyond this weekend. Brad, you're going to have to face going home.''

''Isn't there a place in town that I could rent until I've recovered?''

''Not that I can think of.''

"You could always take me home with you," he suggested in jest.

"Hmm. Something I'd have to think about long and hard," she said over her shoulder as she turned to leave.

"Don't run out on me," he commanded.

"Someone is paging me and you are not my only patient," she replied, frustrated with his stonewalling.

"Why not let him come stay with us?" Jonah asked his granddaughter as she related her difficult day with the obstinate Dr. Jeremiah. "We have that extra bedroom downstairs that no one uses. Besides, I might be able to help."

"You'd like to work with him?" she asked, understanding beginning to dawn.

"It would feel good to get involved again, and I can sorta understand how he feels. It's got something to do with a man's pride. Men like to feel they are in control of their destiny. Right now he feels out of control of every part of his life except where and how he chooses to recuperate."

And so in the end Laura relented. Disregarding her own reservations and the adamant objections of David and Mark, Laura agreed not so much for Brad but rather because of the enthusiasm that had sparked her grandfather's eyes. It was something that had been missing since he'd retired.

So it was that the suave Brad Jeremiah moved into the comfortable old farmhouse over the strong opposition of Mark Harrod and David McBride. However, when David saw his father's pleasure, he relented; Mark, however, adamantly voiced his opposition.

Although apprehension clouded Laura's decision, a strange excitement fluttered her heart as she arrived home to find Brad ensconced in the old swing on the front porch. Gently pushing the swing with his good leg, he greeted her with a warm smile, his eyes peaceful and free of the anxiety that had bound them.

"You're looking chipper, Brad," she acknowledged.

"It feels good to be out of that dungeon. I think your granddad and I are going to hit it off."

A fresh breeze laced with the fragrance of mountain laurel wafted across the porch and ruffled his hair, now long enough to cover his small scar and curling on his neck. He wore one of David's cast-off blue-and-red plaid shirts, open at the collar, along with a pair of the older doctor's jeans.

Laura's heart lurched. He looked anything but the sophisticated doctor she had met in Louisville. Sitting on her porch, relaxed and handsome, he could have inspired a poster for the perfect rugged All-American man.

Disturbed with her emotional response to him, she retorted sharply, "Anyone who can't hit it off with Jonah can't get along with anyone."

A flash of the old Brad flared in his eyes before he drawled, "I've never had a problem before, and I don't anticipate one now."

"How would you know what kind of problem you've had before?"

"I don't. I'm just supposing," he corrected.

"Your first days at the hospital wouldn't support that supposition."

"I definitely was not myself. It must have been a reaction to the medication I was on."

"Whatever it was, you were anything but pleasant."

"Forget the past. Look at me now. All in a good humor, while the lady doctor is testy."

"Don't call me 'lady doctor.'"

"What shall I call you?"

"Must we spar all the time, Brad?"

"That's up to you. I was in a pleasant frame of mind when you arrived. I'm not quite sure what happened. But if 'lady doctor' is the problem, then far be it from me to insult my hostess. If you want to remain formal, then 'Dr. McBride' it will be." He cupped his chin with his hand and grinned at her before adding in a drawl, "'Course, every time I say that I'll think I'm talking to your dad, since nobody else calls you that."

"Okay, just call me 'Laura,' or anything you want to except 'Lady Doctor,'" she snapped, angry with herself for her unreasonable reaction.

"That's more what I had in mind. Seems more sociable somehow." He grinned triumphantly as she retreated through the massive front door.

Chapter Seven

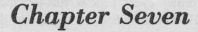

Summer invaded spring and Brad settled comfortably in the old farmhouse. Laura avoided him as much as possible. Occasionally, they took their dinner meal together; more often, she left early for the hospital and stayed late.

Darlene called and vented her fury about Brad's decision, blaming her former suite mate for his refusal to come home. Laura listened patiently to her friend, understanding her frustration, but had no words of encouragement. Brad Jeremiah seemed locked outside the world that was once his. Laura prayed that a breakthrough would come soon.

Laura arrived home one evening to find Jonah and Brad in the old rowboat out in the middle of the pond, fly-fishing. Every now and then, she heard excited exclamations from one or the other as they landed a prize specimen.

When the two finished their adventure just before

twilight, Laura met them on the little makeshift dock. Mud smudged both men's trousers, damp from the leaking old boat, and Brad's hair was tousled and his eyes bright in the early evening light. He held up a string of fish high for her to admire. Suddenly, her last bastion of resistance crumbled as she stood on the sun-warmed, dilapidated landing and peered into the warm brown eyes of the boyish-looking man before her. He had invaded her heart, and despite all inner caution, she liked him.

But it was the light of contentment emanating from her grandfather's eyes that sealed Laura's heart and changed the atmosphere in their home. She grabbed her grandfather's string and teased, "Now I guess you'll want me to cook you some for supper."

"I can't think of anything that would make my day more complete," Jonah replied.

Two hours later the three of them enjoyed a delightful meal.

As Brad finished his after-dinner coffee, he pushed back his chair and fixed his eyes, twinkling with mischief, on Laura. "I'm impressed. Not only can she doctor—she can cook. Is there no end to your accomplishments?"

Laura glanced at her grandfather and blushed, noting that he had not missed the look in Brad's eyes. "I had a good teacher."

"Your mother?"

"Um-hmm, some. But mostly it was Jonah. He taught me how to doctor and to cook."

"What about your dad?"

"He expected me to be a doctor. Jonah taught me how. Dad was and is too busy."

"He's that, all right. I worry about him. Before you know it he'll end up the way I did when I was about his age. 'Course, the Good Lord did that to heal a breach between us," Jonah stated.

"Breach?" Brad asked, his curiosity piqued.

"Even with a strong set of values sometimes we stray. It happened to me. I lost my focus and caused a breach between us."

Brad leaned in toward the silver-haired man, interest sparking his eyes, and inquired, "How was that?"

"I forgot the definition of success."

"I don't understand." Brad shook his head slightly.

"There was a time when I thought success was measured in bank accounts and possessions."

"You don't believe in material wealth?" Brad asked, perplexity written in his wrinkled brow.

Laura stood up from the table and began stacking the plates. "I can see you guys are about to have one of your philosophical discussions, so if you will excuse me to do the dishes and my work, you can continue."

Jonah shook his head, insisting, "Never you mind about the dishes. You run on upstairs." He rose from the table stiffly and began to clear the table.

With Brad's help the kitchen chores were done in record time.

"How about another cup of coffee, Jonah?" Brad asked.

Soon the pleasant aroma of coffee permeated the kitchen and Jonah poured two mugs with the steaming beverage. "What do you say we take it out on the porch and enjoy the cool breeze from the lake."

The sounds of night fell softly on their ears. The chain creaked as Jonah pushed the old swing gently with his foot.

Brad relaxed in the oversize rocker. Suddenly, his voice intruded into the stillness. "Do you believe in material wealth?"

"You mean as the measure of success?" Jonah asked.

"Other than the prestige of accomplishment, I can't imagine how one could measure it any other way, yet you seem to feel that having wealth is wrong," Brad replied, mystified.

"You misunderstood me. I didn't say having material wealth is wrong. It's just not where success is measured."

"If it's not in money, and the accomplishments and prestige it brings, where is it?"

"I believe success is in how you use that wealth. I call it the difference between spending and investing."

"Stock, real estate, etcetera, versus luxury purchases?"

"No. True investing is using your assets to benefit others. You see, dividends on those investments are never subject to the financial market."

"How can that practice benefit you personally?"

"Peace of mind and a sense of purpose. No one can steal them, they can't decay and they live on after we're gone."

"You think the pursuit of wealth will destroy those attributes?"

"When that's your main goal, yes. It always creates an insatiable appetite for more. In the end, some men sacrifice their families, their health and their souls, all in the pursuit of wealth."

"Does it always have to be like that?"

"Afraid so. It's just human nature to lose focus, and when we do, we put at risk all that is dear to us. I almost did, until the Good Lord knocked me flat on my back with a heart attack. Gave me a whole different perspective and set of values."

"I don't see anything wrong with healthy ambition and enjoying the rewards of your labor, plus you gain peace and security from knowing you have profitable investments," Brad argued.

"There's not enough wealth to win peace of mind for a man. The more you have the more you fear losing it. Consequently, the more you sacrifice to keep it."

"If working for financial security and enjoying the luxuries it brings is wrong, what else is there?" Brad stubbornly insisted.

"I never said it was wrong to work hard and enjoy some of the benefits along the way. God designed us to work, and He delights in our enjoyment of His blessings. Our priorities are what interest Him."

"In what way?"

"The question of what motivates our drive. Is it personal ambition or do we have the broader vision of His grand design? Some people are destined for wealth and they have a great responsibility for their use of it. Others, like my son, have a different destiny, one that doesn't include material wealth but the investment of his life into bringing a better life to people.''

''So he is the more noble among us because he denies himself certain privileges?'' A touch of cynicism deepened Brad's voice.

''Nothing of the sort. This is not about nobility but the measure of success. My son is no more or less successful than a wealthy urban physician who is fulfilling God's purpose and place for his life. Nor does his decision make him nobler. Success comes in finding his purpose and then obeying. Only there can one find real peace and security.''

''You said yourself that your son is overworked.''

''Ah, yes, even in fulfilling what you call a 'noble' dream there are temptations and trials.''

Brad Jeremiah chuckled derisively. ''Temptations here?''

''When one forgets from where the dream came and begins to think that it is his alone. The burden becomes too great.''

''Well, whose is it?''

''When it is God who gives us a vision, then He will provide what we need. Right now David has forgotten and is acting as if it were his alone, with no one else to help.''

''From what Laura told me, he is in it alone. Understaffed and undercapitalized, how could he feel any other way?''

''Sometimes God allows us to experience desperation when He is trying to get our attention.''

"I thought He had your son's attention."

"David's heart is right. His vision is myopic at the moment."

"Jonah, you're not making any sense to me."

A warm smile parted Jonah's creased face and his eyes showed merriment. "In simple terms, I think God is trying to redirect my son's life."

"Away from here?"

"I really don't know. I do believe it's time he understood that if the dream is God's dream it will live on beyond him."

"How's that?"

"God has others who would be willing to implement and carry on his vision."

"You mean Laura?"

"Not necessarily. A parent can't dictate and force his dream on his child. I think Laura feels pressure to carry on her father's work simply because she wants to please him, but she'll not be successful until she discovers that his dream is hers, as well. She's not there yet."

"Unless your God gives Laura the vision, then your son is alone, understaffed and undercapitalized, because who in his right mind would come up here and work the way he does for peanuts?"

Jonah looked at Brad for a long moment and said nothing, the quiet in the darkness deafening. Then he asked softly, "Who indeed?"

As Laura's acceptance of Brad grew, life settled into a routine. Laura relaxed and spent pleasant evenings with him and her grandfather. It had been a long time since she had enjoyed herself as much. But she didn't examine her sense of euphoria and, if confronted, would have denied it had anything to do with Brad Jeremiah.

Mark noticed, however, and casually mentioned it to David, who shrugged and admitted he'd had little time to see or think of his daughter of late, much less their difficult patient. He was anxious for Jeremiah to be well and on his way.

Mark couldn't have agreed more. Occasionally, he would drop by the comfortable old farmhouse, then he and Brad would play chess. Laura noticed that, uncharacteristically, Mark seemed aloof and uncomfortable around Laura's houseguest, as if resenting an intrusion into his world.

And indeed it was. As Laura's time increased with Brad, it decreased with Mark. In the past, the affable young man would drop in without notice and enjoyed many impromptu meals with both Laura and Jonah. Of late he had eaten many lonely meals in his cubicle apartment. A stranger now sat at his place at the table and he had seen the way Brad Jeremiah's eyes lingered on Laura. Mark was anything but comfortable with that.

One night he dropped over, to find the two of them sitting on Laura's narrow Victorian love seat, their heads bent so closely together that brown blended with glistening blond. Laura's perfume delicately permeated the air and they shared what seemed to Mark an intimate laugh at something they were looking at in her lap.

Anguish gripped Mark's heart, and he spoke

sharply through the screen door that invited the cool June air in and kept the mosquitoes out. Laura lifted her head, startled, then smiled and invited him in.

Mark returned her smile, but his was stiff, his joy at seeing her snuffed out by the scene before him. "Came by to see if you wanted to go for a soda. I think we have just enough time to make it before the shop closes."

Laura turned to Brad with a questioning look and he shrugged, responding, "Suits me. A soda sounds good."

"Me, too. Anyway, I think you've had enough fun at my expense tonight. Let me freshen up a bit."

Mark nodded, his heart hammering. Having a soda with Brad Jeremiah was not what he'd had in mind. He shoved his hands in his pockets, strolled over and picked up the album Laura had put down.

"She was showing me what it was like growing up in small-town America. Seemed to think it might help jog my memory. I don't know how. According to my records, I've always been an urbanite."

"Yeah, I'd class you a regular city slicker. I guess all this rural life is getting a little tedious for you by now," Mark drawled.

Brad's eyes held Mark's. "Quite the contrary. I find this life fascinating."

"The life or the company?" Mark responded.

"Both."

"How long do you plan to hide out here?"

"Hide out, Harrod?"

"Yes. Avoid reality, refusing to get well," Mark

pressed, disregarding the angry sparks that fired Laura's eyes now that she came back into the room.

"Mark! What are you saying?" she demanded.

Mark jerked his head, his eyes smoldering. "I'm telling the truth. Time somebody did. Dr. Brad Jeremiah is hiding out and he will not recover until he decides he wants to. Which raises even bigger questions. Why doesn't he want to?"

"Mark, this is neither the place nor the time to discuss this," Laura insisted through tight lips.

"I disagree, Laura. Do you want Jeremiah to recover, or are you enjoying this arrangement too much?" Mark retorted, throwing caution to the winds.

"That's enough, Mark," Laura all but shouted.

Meanwhile, Brad watched the exchange with interest and something that bordered on amusement. "Anyone for that soda?" he drawled.

"No, I'm not hungry anymore," Laura snapped.

"Well, I am. Harrod whetted my appetite. You wouldn't want to disappoint your favorite patient, would you?" he implored, an intimate tone in his voice.

"You're not my patient anymore. I dismissed you when you moved into my home," she responded, frustration in her voice, anger still in her eyes.

"Laura's right. Perhaps another night would be better," Mark interjected, having no desire to make it a threesome.

"Nonsense. This fresh mountain air should do us a world of good. Maybe something about it will jog my memory," he teased, his eyes revealing he knew full well he'd gained the upper hand and refused to give ground.

"And if it did, would you keep it to yourself?" Mark demanded.

"You think I'm pretending not to remember?" Brad asked congenially.

"I don't know quite what I think of you, Doctor. You're either pretending or you don't want to get well."

"Mark, you have no right to insult Brad. He is a guest in my home and you will treat him as such," Laura stated, her eyes round with astonishment.

"A fact that I can hardly forget, my dear. Jeremiah, I apologize for my rudeness. I do not rescind my opinions."

"What kind of apology is that?" Laura squealed.

"One I accept," Brad put in smoothly.

"Well, I don't." Laura clamped her jaws shut.

"I didn't apologize to you, Laura. If he accepts it, then you will have to." Mark suddenly grinned, beginning to enjoy himself.

"Well, apologize to me, then," Laura insisted.

"For what?"

"For insulting me."

"I haven't said anything to insult you. My conversation was with Dr. Jeremiah."

"And it was one that intrigues me, I might add," Jeremiah added.

"In what way, may I ask?" Mark smiled despite himself.

"How you came to such a profound medical opinion on my condition."

"Well, this conversation can't be continued here. It definitely calls for a soda. Since Laura doesn't want to go, would you be my guest, Jeremiah?"

"Lead on, Dr. Harrod," Brad said as he turned to follow Mark out the door, leaving a bewildered Laura behind.

Mark kept their conversation light as they each ate their way through a double-dipper hot caramel sundae with nuts and whipped cream. "Good for the heart and the waistline, eh, Doctor?"

"Couldn't agree with you more. How could anything so divine be bad for you? Anyway, you don't seem to have any trouble along those lines."

"Genes, I suppose. You don't seem to have a tendency toward obesity, either."

"I wouldn't know."

"Yeah, that's right. Guess there are quite a few empty gaps."

"Chasms, are more like it."

"You seem to be taking it in stride—in fact, rather enjoying some aspects of it."

"Grates on you, too." Now it was Brad's turn to grin.

"Right. You see, Laura's—" Mark began.

"Your girl," Brad interrupted.

"Thought she was," Mark amended.

"If she were mine I'd make sure of it." Brad smiled, but his eyes flashed a warning.

"Now you're into advising the lovelorn?" Mark quipped, not willing for Brad to see his anguish.

"No, just an observation from an interested bystander."

"How interested?"

"Under other circumstances, I would give you a run for your money. She's too rare a jewel to let her escape."

"But under present circumstances...?"

"I can't afford to get involved." Brad shrugged nonchalantly.

Mark's eyes fired up; his pleasant voice took on an edge. "Laura is not the kind of girl who gets 'involved.'"

"Exactly my point. And anything of a commitment is unthinkable for me at this stage of my life."

"It is?"

"Why, man, I don't even know who I am!" Brad exclaimed, for the first time frustration unmasking his congenial facade.

"Sure you do. You're Dr. Brad Jeremiah, up-and-coming Louisville surgeon," Mark drawled, sarcasm tinging his tone.

"No, I mean really who I am. Contrary to your suspicions, I want to get well, and I remember very little."

"Maybe you just think you want to get well."

"There you go again, Harrod. Just spit it out. You've been trying to all night," Brad responded testily.

"Now who's grating on whom?" Mark smiled his good humor returning.

"Touché. Nonetheless, I would appreciate your getting to the point."

"From the injury you had, you should have suffered only temporary amnesia. This has gone on for months. Either you're an apt pretender or there is something so traumatic that you are subconsciously sealing it off.''

"Now, what could be so terrible that I refuse to recall it?'' Brad asked, denial in his voice and something akin to fear in his eyes.

"I have no idea. Where were you going when you crashed? You filed no flight plan, didn't tell Darlene where you were headed and took off in threatening weather that no reasonable pilot would have flown in. Sounds like a flight of desperation to me.''

Brad stared at Mark, his eyes stormy. "That's your opinion, Doctor.''

"But a valid one.''

"But why would I resist recovering when, as you have suggested, I have the world at my feet?''

Mark paused before answering. His eyes, which held Brad's, were serious, probing, then he observed quietly, "Maybe you suddenly didn't like that world. Or could it be you've found another, more appealing, one?''

Chapter Eight

The old sash groaned as Laura lifted the window and leaned out. Below her, droplets of dew sparkled like diamonds in the early-morning sunlight and the hint of honeysuckle tickled her nostrils. A fresh summer breeze, cooled from a midnight shower, rippled the lace curtains against her bare legs and she breathed deeply, relishing this moment of quiet before the household awakened. As she stretched her arms above her head, a sigh of contentment purred from her innermost being.

Today was her first day off in many weeks, and what a day to be home in these beloved hills. Her eyes caressed them, and now even the azure sky seemed to smile on her as the hills beckoned. Suddenly, visions of a rushing stream, a waterfall and a cool deep pool filled her mind. It took her only a moment to decide, and only minutes to reach that favorite spot.

The sun's brilliance blinded her for a second as she stepped from the darkness of the cave behind the waterfall. Now changed into her swimsuit, she walked the rim of the pool and executed a perfect dive into its cold depths. The water's icy fingers gripped her, shocking her body, hot from the brisk walk through the forest. She broke the surface and gasped, then trod water until she acclimated herself to its coolness. Afterward she swam laps, exhilarating in the refreshing dip.

Played out, the young doctor lay down and napped. When she awakened, she reached in her bag for an apple. It was crisp and sweet, and Laura ate it slowly, savoring the taste and feel of it. An overwhelming sense of peace and contentment seemed to reach out and embrace her on this sun-washed morning.

She laughed aloud. Surely a day off could scarcely be the impetus for such strong and sudden emotion. Then she lay back again, pillowing her head on her towel, and stared upward, as she searched her heart.

Gone were the doubts and questions that had plagued her during and shortly after her trip to Louisville. But just when had they exited? Did it have anything to do with the new direction her career had suddenly taken?

Since Tom's emergency, Laura had noticed an abrupt change in her professional life. Many patients who had previously requested Mark or one of the other part-time physicians now requested "Doc Laura" when they came to the clinic. They had been curious about this lady doctor, Doc Dave's girl and the one who had miraculously saved old Tom's life.

Over hills and down in the valleys the word spread, and soon people from small outlying communities came to see for themselves. And they liked what they found. Her father took notice and gradually relinquished more responsibility to her. Sometimes she caught him looking at her with a touch of pride in his eyes, but with something else, too, that she had yet to define.

She reveled in his approval, which was evidenced by the work he directed her way. As her workload grew, so did her sense of satisfaction, and the doubts that had formerly anguished her dissipated.

In her own mind she had finally settled the question of her ability to handle the awesome responsibility of a physician. But it was more than that. Somewhere along the way God had confirmed in her innermost being that it was here in these hills and hollows she loved that He wanted her to carry out her duties. Now it was not a question of fulfilling her dad's dream, but rather the destiny God had purposed for her. She sighed, held in the cradle of contentment, at peace at last with herself and her destiny.

The inviting warmth of the sun had dried her body and warmed her thoroughly; now the water's coolness looked inviting, and once again she plunged in. Laura swam several more laps around the secluded pool before diving to the bottom once more. When she surfaced this time, she rolled over on her back and made her way to the shore. After pushing up on the rocks, she climbed out and toweled dry on the warm smooth surface.

A voice cut through the morning sounds. "I thought mermaids swam only in the sea."

Laura gazed up into the admiring ebony eyes of Dr. Brad Jeremiah, who lounged against a tree.

Blushing at his scrutiny, she stammered, her heart pounding, "T-to what do I owe this dubious pleasure?"

"I can assure you that my pleasure is not dubious, Dr. McBride," he told her with an impudent grin.

"How long have you been spying on me?" Laura asked, her calm voice failing to betray the confusion rioting inside her.

"Not spying. More like enjoying the scenery. Perhaps I should have called out," he acknowledged.

"That would have been the courteous thing to do."

"But that would have spoiled my surprise."

"What surprise?"

"My rescue-and-revive mission. Jonah sent me up here with a picnic."

"That dear old heart. He makes a career out of taking care of me."

"A rewarding career, I'm sure," Brad responded, a strange look in his eyes.

"He's capable of much more than that, I assure you. But I do enjoy his pampering."

"Well, pamper he did. We have a full-fledged picnic and he commanded you spend the afternoon here, and I agree," Brad offered, still lounging against the tree.

"You do?"

"I want you to show me the other special spots

around here. Why did you keep this glorious place secret?"

"Sometimes when something is so special, you have a hard time sharing it."

"Besides beautiful, what makes it special?"

"Memories."

"Something I'm fresh out of."

"Sorry, Brad. That was a thoughtless remark."

"That's all right. Maybe I can borrow some of yours. They're probably better than mine anyway." He grinned, his mouth crooked, his eyes bright in the morning sunlight. "So am I welcome now?"

Finding his grin infectious, Laura responded, "Your basket is—I'm not sure about you."

"Is that any way to treat a guest?" he teased.

"Guest or intruder—I haven't quite decided," Laura answered, her voice muffled as she slipped an oversize polo shirt over her wet suit.

"After you spend the day with me, you'll count me a treasured guest. By the way, your mom invited us to the big house for dinner. I'm curious how she got the chief to agree to that. I get the distinct impression I'm not one of your dad's favorite people."

"Oh, he's just busy, and not into pampering rich young doctors."

"You think I expect pampering?" Brad asked as he plopped the picnic basket down beside her.

"But definitely," Laura replied with as smile as she peeked in the basket.

Brad threw back his head and laughed. "I think one lady physician at a small community hospital took care of that."

Laura dropped her eyes, unwilling to meet his. "We didn't have a very promising beginning."

"The beginning isn't as important as the ending," he remarked, as he reached out and lifted her chin with his index finger, forcing her to look at him.

Her eyes widened; she was startled at the intimacy she encountered in his. She hesitated before she spoke, desperate to lighten the moment, not knowing, but fearing, where it might lead. Finally she observed, "That depends on the destination."

"What if you have no idea where you're going because you have no idea where you've been?" He dropped his hand; a troubled look dimmed the light in his eyes.

"None yet, Brad?" she asked, sympathy flaring in her eyes.

"Very little. Perhaps that's why I'm holding on to the present so tightly."

"This is only a temporary arrangement. Don't you want to recover?"

"I've asked myself that question over and over. Your boyfriend, Mark, seems to think I don't."

"He's not my boyfriend," Laura denied as she reached into the hamper of food and took out a cloth to spread on a smooth, table-size boulder.

"That's not his impression," Brad noted quietly, and helped unload a container of cold chicken and assorted salads from the ample basket.

"Are you ready to eat? I can't wait another second," Laura said, not meeting his eyes, ignoring his remark.

"Are you kidding? After hauling that basket halfway up a mountain and smelling the fragrance of fresh-baked bread?''

''Good, then let's eat.''

''And talk later?'' he asked.

''All depends. We might be too busy,'' she retorted, still refusing to meet his gaze.

''Busy?'' He quirked an eyebrow.

''Making you a set of memories,'' she hedged with a smile.

They made quick work of the generous meal, and when they had finished, Brad curled up under a shade tree and pillowed his head with a towel a stone's throw away from the ledge where she dangled her feet in the cold pool. ''Mmm. This is the life. Now can we talk?''

''Brad, about that talk...'' She hesitated.

''You'd like to leave some subjects off-limits.''

''Something like that.''

''Like you and Mark.''

''Yes.''

''Why?''

''I'm not sure. Everybody is pushing, questioning, expecting.''

''Mark?''

''No, never Mark. He is the soul of gentleness and consideration.''

''Sounds a lot like me.'' Brad grinned.

''Exactly!'' Laura replied sarcastically. She laughed despite herself.

''You don't think we're similar?'' Brad stood up and moved toward her.

''The only thing I can see that you two have in

common is that you're both physicians," she answered breathlessly, gazing up at him, her whole being suddenly aware of his dark good looks.

With one fluid motion, he dropped to the ledge and faced her, his back to the pool. When he leaned in toward her, his face was so near that she could feel his breath on her forehead, see the rise and fall of his chest. Her heart thundered.

"Do we have you in common?" Brad asked, his tone intimate, his eyes all of a sudden serious.

"I'm not sure what you mean. Mark is my dearest friend. Whereas you are—" She halted; her heart pumped harder.

"I'm what, Laura?" His knowing gaze captured hers, forcing her to see him.

"A new friend?" she offered weakly.

"Just being your friend would not be enough for me," he answered, his voice husky, suddenly full of emotion.

"Then what would?" she inquired, her eyes large in the early-afternoon shadows.

"I'm not sure." He sighed and leaned back, putting some distance between her and him.

"Not sure of what?" she asked, thankful her heart had slowed.

"Of me." He closed his eyes as if to shut the world away.

"Your emotions, you mean?" she delved.

"Oh, lady, my memory may not be in working order, but my emotions are at full throttle." He chuckled mirthlessly, then added, "Especially when I'm around you."

"Brad, this is just an interlude. The real world is out there somewhere, waiting for you to pick up the pieces of your life."

"The way you make me feel is not a fantasy."

"Your emotions are heightened. They're not dependable." She told herself as well as him.

"Mark suggested that I haven't recovered because I don't want to."

"Mark wasn't himself that night."

"Perhaps he's right. Maybe I don't want to go back to where I was."

"Oh, Brad, don't you see? This is a brief escape from a world that had, for some reason, become too complicated for you."

"You don't understand, Laura. It's not returning to a complicated world that I'm afraid of." His eyes burned into hers, daring her to turn away. Willing her to look into the very windows of his soul.

He leaned closer and she asked, "Then what are you afraid of, Brad?"

Like a camera in slow motion, Laura watched helplessly as his head bent lower. Cupping her face in his hands, he lifted it as his mouth covered hers in a tender kiss. Her heart pounded a response that reached her lips, betraying all her resolve. When finally he lifted his head and released her, they both trembled.

A tremulous smile played around his mouth as he answered in a husky voice, "Of losing you."

Suddenly he reached out and enfolded her in his arms. Cradling her head in the curve of his shoulder, he crushed her to him as if he'd never let her go.

The world outside remained silent, while their

hearts sang in unison an age-old refrain. Then he loosened his hold on her and lifted his head. Her eyes were closed. Two lonely tears trickled down her cheeks. Still she did not speak. A shudder racked him, and with his fingertips, he brushed the tears away and kissed her forehead, then her eyes, her cheeks, and finally his lips claimed hers once more.

What began gently grew more intense as Laura's arms moved up to encircle his neck. Her hard-won resistance to this mysterious stranger suddenly evaporated and she gave herself to the kiss. When at last common sense returned, Laura pushed against him and he released her, his eyes questioning.

"This will never do," she whispered, her voice breaking.

"Why? How can you deny what just happened? You felt the same as I did."

"My emotions are no different, Brad, only my values."

"What do you mean by that?" he asked, irritation sparking in his eyes.

"Destination."

"Destination?" he spit, his breath still ragged.

"Yes, where what just happened will lead, I'm not prepared to go."

"Is that some kind of self-righteous mumbo jumbo?" he snarled, anger darkening his face.

"No. A long time ago I determined what was right for me."

"And that is?"

"Lifetime commitment." Her words cut through the summer silence.

"How can I commit for a lifetime, when I don't even know what my life is?" he railed, closing his hand into a fist.

"You can't and neither can I. That's why it's wrong."

"Wrong to feel the way we do?"

"The feeling is not wrong. The expression of it can be disastrous."

"For whom?"

"For both of us," she stated softly.

"But I love you," he insisted, clenching his teeth.

"Do you love me or want me, Brad? Big difference." She smiled sadly. "The only thing this afternoon proved is that we have an explosive attraction between us, but I won't confuse that with love."

"How do you know what love is?"

"I know that it's more than two bodies wildly attracted to each other. It begins with friendship, compatibility."

"I think we have that."

"Perhaps. Then it grows into admiration and respect, where thoughts, ideas, values and aspirations are shared."

"But you have all that with Mark, yet you deny being his girl."

"If you are trying to persuade me Mark's the one for me, then join the crowd."

"So far he fits the bill and I fail the test."

"You haven't failed any test, Brad. I don't know you well enough to make those determinations about you."

"I don't know myself. How do I know if I'm someone with admirable qualities?"

"Or that we share the same set of values?" she noted gently.

"It still sounds like good old Mark will win fair maiden," he retorted, cynicism lacing his voice. "What else defines this thing you call love?"

"I think it involves being willing to place someone else's happiness above my own."

"What about enjoyment, excitement—are those not important elements?" he drawled, anger extinguished now, a tentative approval in his eyes.

She laughed, blushing. "Oh, yes. It's knowing that you'd rather be with someone more than anyone else in the world. And as far as excitement goes, I think my granddad put it best when he said my grandmother turned the morning on for him."

Brad's dark eyes misted. "She's been gone all these years, and he still says that?"

She nodded. "And although my dad has never said those exact words, it's in his eyes every time my mother enters a room. Those are the benefits of that thing called 'a sacred commitment.' I determined a long time ago I'd settle for nothing less."

"What about us, what just happened?" he asked.

"Only time will tell, Brad."

"Time? How much?"

"However long it takes to get to know each other," she replied her voice husky with emotion.

"Meanwhile, Mark—"

"Or Darlene. You never know what will happen

when you regain your memory,'' she reminded him gently.

"There is nothing in this world or the world to come that could change the way I feel about you. I mean to have you, Laura McBride.''

Chapter Nine

After his initial anger, Brad regained his charm. They spent the afternoon wading in the streams that abounded in the forest, laughing and having water fights. He encouraged Laura to share her memories with him and she did, offering her yesterdays up to him as an investment in their uncertain tomorrows. And he listened, enchanted.

They arrived back at Laura's in the late afternoon with just enough time to dress for her parents' dinner. Parting in the kitchen to go to their rooms, Brad reached over and placed a whisper-soft kiss on her forehead. "When my memory returns, today will still be the most treasured I possess."

Laura eyes widened in surprise. "All of it?"

"Every second of it," he said with a grin, and she blushed profusely beneath her sun-kissed face.

Now they walked quietly up the tree-lined pathway leading to her parents' house. Both seemed to be in a world of their own. Yet an occasional surreptitious glance, one toward the other, betrayed their thoughts.

Laura's halter dress of navy linen set off her willowy figure, ending modestly midcalf. Brad towered over her, his dark good looks the perfect complement to her fragile blond beauty. His white sport coat, worn over a navy open-collar shirt, was cut expertly, thanks to a local tailor. As he leaned down to reach around her for the doorbell, he encompassed her in his arms, and memories of this afternoon beside the waterfall flooded her mind. Laura was flushed and distracted when her mother opened the door.

Brad smiled smoothly, noting Laura's discomfort and her mother's scrutiny. "This must be the lovely lady I've heard such heroic tales about," he observed, gently moving Laura to one side as he reached for Cassie McBride's hand.

Laura stammered, "M-mom, this is Dr. Brad Jeremiah. Brad, Cassie McBride."

The charming woman with saucy dark hair sprinkled with silver bit one lip, trying to hide the smile that threatened to erupt. Her large mahogany eyes, wise and discerning, glittered with amusement.

"Well, I finally get to meet you, Dr. Jeremiah. I've heard so much about you."

"Mrs. McBride, please don't form your opinions on hearsay." He laughed, completely at ease.

"Oh, don't worry, I make up my own mind, based solely on what I know to be facts," Cassie answered with her most charming smile.

"You're most gracious, despite the infamous tales I'm sure you've heard," Brad complimented her.

"Now, who would be carrying tales, Jeremiah?" interrupted a somewhat gruff voice from across the room.

"Oh, good evening, sir. I didn't say they were undeserved—just infamous," Brad smoothly countered as his eyes met the piercing blue ones of his host, Laura's father.

"Oh, don't mind, David. His bark is worse than his bite," Cassie warned as she went over to her husband.

David took his wife's hand and moved across the room to extend his right hand to Brad. "Welcome, Jeremiah, good to have you over. I see you're walking quite well." The older doctor narrowed his eyes. "How's your other problem progressing?"

"Oh, flashes of memory now and then."

"Can't imagine why it's taking so long to recover. You didn't suffer a brain injury, only some pressure, which I relieved, from the internal bleeding."

"I'm thankful for that, Dr. McBride. You saved my life and I'm most grateful."

"It was an emergency decision we had to make, Jeremiah. Pressure was rising quickly and we didn't have time to wait to get anyone's permission. Dangerous situation."

"I'm well aware of that, Dr. McBride. Your decision took a lot of courage."

"I'm glad it was a simple problem to fix once I went in. I'm still at a loss about why you haven't recovered your memory. 'Course, amnesia's not my field. Now, if it were a lung problem, well, that's my specialty."

"Harrod has a theory about it that I'm considering. Meanwhile, I've determined to be patient and accept life on a day-to-day basis." Brad's eyes left David's and caressed Laura's face, a smile playing around his mouth.

Cassie McBride's discerning eyes darted from her daughter to her guest, then held Laura's and winked.

Brad was at his charming best throughout the meal and Laura watched the ice in her father's blue eyes melt, their characteristic sparkle return. David seemed as if a great weight had suddenly lifted off him, and for the first time in weeks, the deep lines between his eyes eased and he relaxed.

Brad quizzed him on his work, the clinic, his aspirations and the problems he encountered. What had begun as polite conversation ended with David inviting the young doctor to go up into the hills with him and assist him on some house calls. "Perhaps it will stir your remembrance a bit."

The younger doctor responded with enthusiasm, "I'd love the opportunity, sir. Maybe I can tell if my skills are locked away with my memory or if they're just lying there dormant."

"My thoughts exactly."

David leaned forward, his face alight with excitement, as it always was when he discussed his work. Cassie watched her husband, pride and relief illuminating her liquid brown eyes.

"At any rate, sir, I could drive for you. I haven't forgotten how, and my leg is in fine shape," Brad offered.

"You'll have to get up early. I make about a hundred-mile junket each time," David warned.

"How often do you go?"

"Once a week regularly, then any additional emergency calls."

"And run the hospital, too?"

"With very little time for anything else." Cassie laughed, a light, melodious sound.

"Don't you resent all that time away from you?" Brad turned his dark eyes on Laura's mother.

Cassie's smile was warm as she responded, "Resentment is a waste of time and emotion. It would only serve to spoil what time we do have together, time too precious to waste."

"You're quite a woman, Mrs. McBride," Brad replied in an admiring tone.

Cassie looked at her husband, then back at Brad. "No, I've got quite a man. And I'm committed to him and to his work. He is his work. They are inseparable, I accepted that when I married him. If God should choose, at some point in our lives, to give us more time together, I'll rejoice in it. Until then, I cherish each moment that we have."

"Well, dear, you never can tell what God might have in store for us." David's eyes twinkled at his wife, a mysterious smile playing around his mouth.

"Some new financing come in to ease our situation at the hospital?" Laura asked.

"No, the problems are still the same. Mark Harrod graciously reminded me who's in control of them," David admitted.

"Harrod seems Johnny-on-the-spot giving advice lately," Brad drawled, his eyes hooded.

David turned his full attention to Brad, a questioning look on his face. He replied evenly, his gaze explicit, "Mark's a good man. He zeros in on the truth and then has the courage to state it. I admire that in any man."

"Well, I've encountered a little of that myself, Dr. McBride. Everything I've heard about him points to an honorable man," Brad reluctantly agreed, as his glance shifted to Laura.

"Yes, an honorable man—a rare treasure in today's world." The older doctor emphasized the word "rare," as he let his gaze drift away from Brad to rest on Laura. An unmistakable message passed from father to daughter.

Sensing the tension, Cassie McBride smoothly remarked, "A treasure recognized is a delight, but I'm sure that we stay so busy that we often miss others right under our noses. Now, Dr. Jeremiah, I can't tell you what an answer to prayer you are to me. Just think, David will have company and someone to share his workload. Why, he should get home twice as quickly!"

"I don't know if my skills will be beneficial to him, but I am excited about the possibility. I consider it a privilege to observe a physician of Dr. McBride's stature."

David put the journal he was reading on the bedside table and watched his wife enter the room. As always, the very sight of her thrilled him. The thrill had never diminished. His love and enjoyment of her were constants in his life.

She seemed to float across the room. A gown and peignoir of periwinkle enhanced her dark beauty, and a mysterious smile played around the full, rosy lips he loved to kiss. Age had only enhanced her grace and loveliness. The sacrifices and sorrows of life had served to forge an inner strength and beauty that no amount of cosmetics could duplicate. Tonight her eyes sparkled in the lamplight, excitement turning them luminous as she came to him.

Cassie sat down on the bed and perched in the curve of his body as he turned to face her. She looked up into his face. "David, what did you mean, we might have more time together?"

"Um, I don't know. Something Mark suggested," he murmured as he planted a kiss on her cheek.

"Dav—id, I already know that. I want to know what Mark said," Cassie persisted, leaning into his kiss.

"Do you know you talk too much, Cassie?" David murmured, obviously not interested in conversation.

"That's because you don't tell me enough, David McBride. I have to pull it out of you like a dentist pulling teeth." She sat straight up, her back rigid, an enchanting smile tempering her words.

David chuckled and hauled himself upright in bed. "All right. I give up. When your curiosity is stirred, there's no anything until it's satisfied. You are one focused woman."

"I had a good teacher, my dear." She leaned over and cupped his cheek with her hand.

"Cassie, that is not the way to continue this discussion," he warned with a smile, emotion darkening his eyes.

"Okay, I'll keep my distance. Just tell me before I burst."

"Seems Mark thinks I ought to expand my horizons," David murmured, tracing the top of her shoulder with his finger.

"How?" Cassie asked, placing her hand over his.

"Mark suggested that I take advantage of some of these speaking engagements to expand our sphere of influence and while I am at it let you organize my notes and write about our experiences in this area."

She sat up, alert, enthusiasm shining in her eyes. "I would consider it my greatest privilege to be a small part of your work."

"As Brad Jeremiah said, what a woman!" His eyes held hers, and an intimate look passed between them that brought a flush to her cheeks.

"I aim to please, Dr. McBride," she responded demurely, finally tearing her gaze from his.

"'Please' hardly scratches the surface." He grinned and reached for her.

Wrapped in his arms, she snuggled closer to him and asked dreamily, already anticipating time with him, "What about the hospital while your off and about?"

"Mark said God would provide someone here if He is redirecting my life."

"Wise young man," she murmured against his lips as he placed a whisper-soft kiss on hers.

"You know, I think Mark might be in love with

Laura. He would be the perfect match for that daughter of ours. Together they could carry on here," David said, smiling down on the woman in his arms.

"Is Papa thinking of arranging a marriage for our daughter?" Cassie pushed away from him to stare up into his face, round-eyed with disbelief.

David took her hand. "Of course not. It's just a matter of time before she comes to her own conclusions about him."

"David, what makes you think she hasn't already?" Cassie asked, an edge to her voice.

"As I said, it's only a matter of time. I've observed them together. He's crazy about her."

"One doesn't make a couple, David."

"Why wouldn't she want him? It's time Laura started thinking about settling down." David's voice rose a decibel; he was as exasperated as always when his wife didn't agree with him.

"Don't you think it's for your daughter to decide that?" Cassie asked, refusing to be convinced.

"Sometimes people need a little encouragement."

"You wouldn't dare."

"Don't you like Mark?"

"I love Mark. He's everything I would have wanted our son to be," Cassie declared.

"Well, then, what's wrong with him for your daughter?"

"What if she doesn't love him, David?"

"What's there not to love about Mark? He's the most honorable young man I know, not to mention his skill as a physician, and he's crazy about Laura. You should have seen him when I criticized Laura the other day. Jumped right in and stood up to me, his boss, in her defense. I tell you I was impressed. No question, he'd make her a fine husband." David nodded as if the decision were already made.

"I have no disagreement with you there, darling. It's Laura's making him a wife that concerns me," she suggested gently.

"Laura would make a good wife for any man. Look what a role model she had," David reminded her with a winning smile.

"Laura doesn't love Mark in the same way I loved you."

"Why do you say that?"

"She's fallen in love with Brad Jeremiah."

"She's what?" David all but shouted.

"You heard me, darling." Cassie answered softly but firmly.

"That man is not the right one for her. She'll make a wreck of her life," he railed.

"And Mark is?"

"In my opinion, he is. She's just got to be convinced, and you're the one to do it."

"I'll do nothing of the sort." Cassie lifted her chin, a sure sign she'd not be persuaded.

"Why? Do you want Brad Jeremiah to marry her and take her away from here?" David demanded, anger and fear firing the blue in his eyes.

"David, I want for Laura the joy I've experienced loving you, being your wife. If it means Brad Jeremiah, then so be it. Can you actually say you'd not want her to have what we have?"

David McBride looked into his wife's eyes, suddenly humbled by the love he saw there. He gathered her into his arms. In a husky voice he answered, "No, my darling. How could I ever deny my daughter the rapture I've known with you?"

He placed a long, slow kiss on his wife's lips, then murmured against her cheek, as he reached to turn out the light, "But I can always hope it turns out to be Mark, can't I?"

Cassie giggled in the darkness and turned to her husband.

Chapter Ten

The old Land Rover climbed the terrain like a sure-footed mountain goat. Although its battered body evidenced the years of abuse the rugged trail had given it, the old engine purred, powering the two doctors up the steep, rutted trails without complaint.

Brad sat in silence, awed by the primitive beauty that lay before him. Like an opening curtain, the dawn-illuminated valley and mountain draped in a filmy gown of early mist. On one side of the trail, scarcely wider than a car's breadth, a giant granite bluff towered above them, while on the other, hardly more than a few steps from the door he clutched, the valley spread out a thousand feet beneath them. A river divided the valley, winding like a ribbon, catching the morning light, before disappearing in the mist. He lowered his window, and the musty smell of damp forest, mingled with the faint fragrance of wood smoke, drifted into the car. He looked out and spied a thin column of smoke on the mountain above him. A cabin he reckoned, and someone was cooking breakfast. Suddenly, his stomach rumbled a complaint. He was hungry.

"Dr. McBride, has your wife ever been on these calls with you?"

"Many times. She's done quite a bit of her research for her stories on these trips with me."

"No wonder she worries about your safety. The trip is a challenge in itself."

"You get accustomed to it. I hardly think about it," David said, his mind already on the cases ahead.

Brad looked at him and raised his brow, then shook his head. "Why do you make these calls? Why not have people come to you?"

"The ones who can do, but more lack transportation. These are not two-car middle-class families, you know." David smiled, knowing Brad could hardly envision what was in store for him.

"I thought you were here to study the miners and lung disease. It seems to me that serving these mountain people would have no benefit to your research," Brad observed, a puzzled look on his face.

"You're right. They are two separate projects, except when those few who work in the mines contract lung ailments."

"Then why do you waste time on these long trips? Once a week you said—that's a lot of your time."

"I don't consider it a waste of time, Brad. They have been my first duty, the research secondary."

"Surely the research would reach further and prove

much more lucrative.'' Brad shook his head, uncomprehending.

"I can't say that some nights when I come in late and exhausted I'm not tempted to give up this part of my practice." David chuckled, then added, a faraway expression in his eyes, "But then I remember why I came in the beginning."

"What decided you on this work?" Brad asked.

"You could say I was drawn here."

"How so?"

"Do you believe in God, Brad?" David inquired.

"I suppose so," Brad murmured without conviction.

"In order to understand why I'm bouncing around these mountains at dawn in a fifteen-year-old vehicle, on my way to make a house call to someone who will pay me in turnip greens, you have to understand something of what dictates my choices."

"Now, are you going to tell me God dictates your choices? You sound like Jonah," Brad quipped.

"I guess it runs in the family." David's smile was patient as he continued, groping for the right words. "'Dictates' is too strong a word, I think. In a way I'm saying that my aim is to let God guide me in all my decisions."

"In an audible voice or a vision?" Brad asked, cynicism creeping into his voice.

David laughed. "Personally, I've never heard an audible voice that I recognized as God's."

"Then how did He communicate to you?" Brad wanted to know, an eyebrow arched quizzically

"God first spoke through my heart."

"So how did you know it was God?" Brad queried, reluctant to accept David's statement.

"It started with a deep longing for something I couldn't define. All I knew was that I was deeply dissatisfied with life as it was," David explained, glancing from the narrow trail to look directly at Brad.

"So you haven't always known a lot about God?" Brad questioned a glimmer of hope touching his eyes as he squirmed in his seat.

"No, I was too busy to give Him much thought," David admitted.

"So what happened?"

"I haven't always lived like this." David's mouth parted in a patient smile and he waved toward his jalopy. "Once, I had all the trappings of success. Engaged to a beauty queen, drove an expensive car, was a member of the country club, vacationed in all the hot spots, had an unlimited prosperous business future in my dad's practice in Kansas. And was totally miserable. Through that misery, God got my attention."

"How did you get from there to here?"

"A group of local physicians were going on a mission trip to set up a temporary clinic in this area. I didn't want to go, but something in their eyes, their demeanor, drew me. They seemed to have a sense of purpose and destination that I lacked."

"Surely you had set goals for yourself."

"I had goals but no sense of fulfillment. Every goal that I attained only left an emptiness that seemed to say, is this all there is? What next?"

Brad nodded, as if something David had said hit a mysterious, responding chord.

David continued. "Spending two weeks with them forced me to do a lot of soul-searching. After several miserable nights, I came to the conclusion that I wanted in my life whatever it was those doctors had discovered."

"You're trying to tell me it was doing charity work that made them happy?"

"No, I'm not, Brad. I discovered that they had found joy and contentment through their faith."

"What kind of faith can do that?"

"A faith in the God who designed me. When I realized that He also had a special design for my life, I found the purpose and fulfillment that had been missing. Turned out it was here in the very hills where first He had gotten my attention."

"Being real religious is not for everyone, you know," Brad remarked after an awkward silence.

David braked, then turned his eyes from the narrow road and fastened them on the young doctor squirming in the seat beside him. "Brad, being religious is not the point. Every man has an emptiness that only God can fill. The question everyone has to answer to ultimately is will he choose to let God fill it?"

"When I consider what you've given up, it seems that you serve a demanding master," Brad answered obstinately.

"I see it as an opportunity to experience a harmony in my life that can only come when I do what He created me to do. The by-product is peace, contentment and joy, even in the midst of the most trying circumstances,'' David responded.

"Sorry, but when I look at your life, the sacrifices you make seem to outweigh the advantages. I'm not quite willing to give up my dreams and goals for anyone. That is when I rediscover what mine were."

"Believe me, Brad, life has a way of making you willing," said David, and laughed.

The afternoon sun rested on the horizon as David and Brad Jeremiah bounced down the last mountain trail before returning to the highway that led home. The two, encased in their own thoughts, had scarcely spoken for the past couple of hours.

David mulled over his earlier conversation with Jeremiah and doubt teased his mind as he questioned who would care for this invisible horde, hidden by the crevices and peaks of the Appalachian Mountains, after he was gone. Mark had said God would send someone. David had hoped it would be Mark and Laura, but if Cassie was right, there would be no Laura and Mark to carry on in his stead. Maybe Laura and this Jeremiah? Unthinkable. The very thought of her choosing Jeremiah racked his soul with worry.

And what about this Jeremiah? David frowned, searching his heart. What had he hoped to accomplish and why? He knew. The sooner Jeremiah recovered, the sooner he'd return home. And David wanted him out of Laura's life. But then, did he have the right to feel as he did? A sense of helplessness washed over him.

He sighed. He might try it again. He needed more

time to get to know this man. Try to see what Laura saw in him. He smiled sadly, aware Cassie would approve his attempt. Then shook his head slightly, as though trying to clear his mind. How could she be so trusting? His smile reached his eyes and he cast an eye toward his companion. It wasn't Laura's emotions or her ability to decide that Cassie trusted, but the One into whose Hands she had relinquished her daughter long ago. David struggled. Could he do the same?

Brad stirred beside him, as if he could read David's thoughts. "I think there is someone on the side of the mountain. He's trying to get our attention."

David braked to an abrupt halt and swung out of the Rover, yelling over the top, "Simon, what is it?

"Jenny? She's in labor? Climb in," David invited as he plopped behind the wheel and backed into a shallow cut in the bank. Maneuvering the vehicle with care, he turned the car around on the narrow road and started back up the mountain.

Darkness curtained the last fingers of light in the western sky, and the stars twinkled in a velvet sky. Brad Jeremiah sat on the floor of the Lovetts' front porch, his feet resting on the large boulder that served as a lone step between the rough hewn porch and the red rocky clay ground. Occasionally, a whimpering sound came from the bedroom lean-to that housed Jenny Lovett and her husband, Simon.

They had arrived three hours before to find Jenny in hard labor a good month before her baby was due. Despite her being racked with pain, her soft cloud of

corn-silk hair, which hung in damp ringlets from perspiration, framed a face of fragile, unearthly beauty
that seemed out of place in the harshness of her surroundings. Her large eyes, wide set and the color of
a summer sky, filled with relief at the sight of David
McBride, trust replacing fear.

Now David worked feverishly to fulfill that trust,
but with each ongoing hour, success appeared less
likely. The flickering lamp cast shadows on his face,
which was lined with fatigue as he stepped out on the
porch for a breath of air. The whimpering inside
reached a crescendo when a scream cut through the
night sounds and David turned to go back in. Brad
stood and stretched, then followed him inside.

"Brad." David met him at the door, a soft urgency
in his voice. "The baby is under stress. It is breach
and the heartbeat has slowed to a dangerous level.
Jenny cannot have this baby on her own."

"Well, what can you do?" Panic touched Brad's
eyes.

"I'll have to perform a cesarean," David announced simply and firmly.

"Here?" Brad all but shouted.

"Yes, here, and you're going to have to assist."

"I can't assist. I don't remember how," Brad protested

"You'll have to. And we don't have time to ar-
gue." David had already turned on his heel and
started for the lean-to.

"What about anesthesia?"

"I have a sedative in my satchel and I can give her

a local. I told Simon, and he's sterilizing my equipment and her bed.''

"What have you told the patient?"

"That we have no choice."

"And what did you tell her about your assistant?"

"That you are a well-known and capable Louisville trauma surgeon who has performed many cesareans."

"How do you know?"

"You were an intern and resident—you did perform cesareans."

"Did you tell her I don't remember how?"

"Of course not. She's scared enough already. Now, let's scrub up."

"There's one thing I have to say for you, Dr. David McBride. Given the occasion, your actions are bold and decisive," Brad declared, a reluctant admiration flaring in his eyes.

"If a doctor allows fear to motivate him, he can do nothing. If we do nothing we'll lose our patient. At least we can give her a chance. We've wasted enough time. Come on," David said in a no-nonsense tone.

A rigid Brad Jeremiah stood by David's side as the older physician deftly moved the scalpel through skin and tissue. A bright stream of crimson blood erupted, and without thinking, Brad took the readied sponges and mopped as David cut. As if in a dream, he clamped arteries and with forceps pushed aside obstructions. They worked in unison. With fluid motions Brad anticipated a need and acted without David ever voicing a command. Within a few seconds, David reached his objective and a weak but welcome cry came from a small baby girl, whom he gently placed on the chest of a quietly sleeping Jenny Lovett.

David turned to Brad. "Dr. Jeremiah, you finish up the sutures. I need to introduce Simon Lovett to his daughter."

As though in a dream, Brad Jeremiah completed the surgery with skill and speed just as the young mother opened wide and frightened eyes.

One question fell from slurred lips. "My baby?"

Brad Jeremiah's smile lit the room, and his dark eyes glowed with relief and joy. "A fine baby girl, Jenny. Your husband is making her acquaintance."

Simon spoke from the door as he entered the room, a blanket bundled in his arms. "She's beautiful, just like you, my Jenny."

Brad's eyes misted as he watched the love in the mountain man's eyes as he tenderly wiped the ringlets from his wife's forehead and laid their daughter in her arms. She smiled as a tiny hand clasped the finger she put in it.

"Amanda," she replied softly, and snuggled the baby closer as she drifted off to sleep.

"How can I ever thank you for what you did for my Jenny and Amanda tonight?"

"Just doing our job, Simon," David murmured, now that the crisis was over; his face was drawn in lines of fatigue.

"Jenny and the baby had a close call. Had Dr. Jeremiah not been with me, things might not have turned out so well. Simon, Jenny is too frail to have any more children. Do you understand what I mean?" David asked, his tone commanding.

"I understand now, Doctor. Since I saw what my Jenny went through and how I nearly lost her, I realized that just because my mother had twelve boys don't mean Jenny can."

"That's right. Your mother didn't have a severe case of rheumatic fever when she was three that left her heart damaged."

"Thank you again, Doctor. Sure wish I had something to repay you with," Simon sputtered.

"Next fall when you go hunting, bring me a turkey. We'll roast him for Thanksgiving." David's mouth parted in a tired smile.

"I'll sure be a-doin' that, Dr. Dave," he promised, relieved.

As David and Brad headed out to the Rover, the flashlight's narrow beam illumined the steep path back to the vehicle. David was moving toward the driver's side, when Brad volunteered, "Dr. McBride, would you let me drive? I'll take it slow and easy."

"Jeremiah, sounds great—and how about calling me 'David'?"

"I would consider it an honor, sir."

"And drop the 'sir.' I believe that after what we've just been through together, we could consider ourselves colleagues."

"It was a surprising turn of events, now wasn't it, s—David?" Brad corrected himself, relishing the camaraderie David offered. For the first time in many months he felt he belonged. A sense of satisfaction settled around him like a warm bath and he acknowledged to himself that he had contributed to the day's success. Somewhere within, hope stirred.

Brad stepped onto the porch and the light came on. Jonah and Laura both waited at the door, anxiety written on their faces.

"Where have you been? Run into trouble? Old Bessie quit on you?" Laura demanded, relief lighting her eyes.

"No, my lady, it wasn't car trouble but doctoring that kept us up in them thar hills, and I do mean hills."

Brad ate his supper belatedly and drank almost a pot of coffee, and his eyes glowed with excitement as he relayed to Jonah and Laura the adventures of the day. He described his uneasiness when David began to see patients. He shared with them the disappointment he felt when his memory failed to budge and his eagerness to leave. Then he described the crisis at the Lovett home and how David had forced him to assist. "There was nothing else he could do. He had to have help, and when I saw his scalpel cut flesh, it was as if something unlocked inside me and I had all this knowledge and skill just waiting to be called up. I remembered and reacted without even having to concentrate on what I was doing."

"Did anything else come back to you, Brad?" Jonah probed eagerly.

"No. Just my skills. Of course, I was too busy to consider anything but what was at hand. Perhaps tonight..."

"What about coming home? Surely on the drive home."

"I drove down that mountain in a fog. All my attention was on the road."

"Sounds as if you had a very successful day. You should be satisfied with the outcome."

"'Satisfied' is not quite the word for it."

"'Exciting'?"

"It went much deeper than that. When I knew that young woman would survive and David placed that baby in her arms, I was filled with awe. I felt humble to have been part of the process of bringing a life into the world." His eyes misted with emotion as he added, "I know one thing. When I return to my practice, I'll have a new perspective."

"Return, Brad?" Laura asked, her heart jolting.

He nodded, and an unspoken message passed between them, then he explained. "Very soon. I think I'm ready to face whatever I've been running from."

"So you agree with Mark," Laura stated quietly, an unreasonable fear gripping her.

"His assessment has to be correct. My skill level was there this afternoon, so my problem has to be an emotional block of some sort. I can't go on with my life until I settle it." He fastened his eyes on Laura, who blushed and dropped her gaze. "And I want to get on with my life."

"When do you plan to leave?" Jonah asked, lips pursed thoughtfully.

"I'll call Darlene tomorrow and tell her what happened, then I'll find out when she wants me back." He chuckled. "I'm sure yesterday wouldn't have been too soon, in view of the flack she gave Laura."

Jonah put his hands on the massive old table, pushed himself up and hobbled toward the sink, coffee cup in hand. "These old bones are calling for bed, young folks. If you'll excuse me, I'll see you two in the morning.''

After Jonah left the room, Brad walked over to Laura. Turning her toward him, he picked up her hand and kissed it. His voice grew husky. "Laura, I knew yesterday that I wanted to go on with my life. Whatever I have to face I'm willing, if I can have you.''

Laura drew back, her eyes wide, her pupils large and dark in her pale face. "Brad, nothing has changed since yesterday.''

"Everything has changed. I have recovered my skills, and I found my future—you.''

"Oh, Brad," Laura moaned, reluctant to dampen the day's victories but unwilling to give him false hope. "Don't say that.''

"You can't say you feel nothing for me," Brad declared, his eyes demanding the truth from hers.

"You know I can't," she admitted, a sad smile curving her lips. "But a relationship is built on more than feelings.''

"That's a beginning.''

"Emotions fluctuate, sometimes fool.''

"There's nothing foolish or unstable about the way I feel about you.''

"Nor I you. But there is so much more required of a relationship before it can even begin to be successful.''

"Perhaps you expect too much.''

"I will settle for nothing less than one that will last a lifetime. There are necessary ingredients that we lack at this point.''

"Such as?''

"I told you yesterday. Friendship, respect, shared goals and values."

"We're friends, I trust when I regain my identity there will be something to respect. And as for shared goals and values, surely that won't pose a problem. I have no problem with my wife having a successful career. Seems to have worked exceptionally well with your parents."

She hesitated, not wanting to ruin the hope that the day had offered him. "Brad, the main ingredient is missing."

"And what can that be?" His countenance darkened; apprehension touched his eyes, turning them coal black.

"A shared faith."

"A what?"

"Brad, I happen to believe that the only true foundation for a successful marriage is a shared faith in God."

"I'm sure there are a lot of good and respected men with reasonably happy marriages who aren't religious giants," Brad snapped, resisting her words.

Laura laughed sadly. "I don't want a religious giant."

"Then what do you want?" he asked, his voice softening, his eyes searching for a reason to hope.

"I want someone whose life view is dictated by his faith."

"What does that have to do with us, marriage?"

"Our belief system dictates our goals and values. Without the foundation of a genuine faith, there is nothing on which to base decisions, goals or values.

Marriage is more than passionate emotions. It's a commitment to weather the storms of life together. Only a genuine shared faith can do that.''

"Who's to say I don't believe in God?''

Laura laughed sadly. "To acknowledge He exists is only the beginning, Brad.''

"Is it enough to give me hope, Laura?'' he pleaded.

"To pretend you possess what you don't would only bring about disaster.''

"Are you saying that there is no chance for us, Laura?'' Brad grabbed her shoulders. "I won't accept that.''

"I don't know what God has in mind. But this one thing I do know. You are not here by accident, nor did you lose your memory coincidentally. It happened by design. When circumstances warrant, I believe your heart will desire to know the Designer. Only then will genuine faith begin. It won't happen in order to please or win me but in response to a deep need in your own life.''

"Until then?''

"We'll wait.''

Chapter Eleven

Brad joined Laura in the sunny breakfast nook as she finished her final cup of tea. He poured a cup of rich dark coffee, the aroma filling the room, and sat down beside her, a perplexed look wrinkling his brow.

Laura smiled; her eyes questioned; yet she remained quiet, not willing to intrude.

When he looked up, he grinned, uncertainty still sparking his dark eyes. "I called Darlene."

"I'd wager 'glad' doesn't describe her reaction to your news. 'Ecstatic' would be more like it," Laura observed dryly.

"As a matter of fact, 'cordial,' 'cooperative' and 'subdued' would more nearly describe her response," Brad corrected, shaking his head in puzzlement.

"What did you tell her?"

"That I had regained my skills but just bits and snatches of memory of my personal life, and that I

would like to come to Louisville, visit my apartment
and the hospital and see if this jogged my memory,
then go to work.

"She suggested that I stay a while longer and work
with you in the hospital here until I gained my confidence and was sure of my skill level. She thinks it
might not be good for our practice if I see patients
before I regain my memory."

"What happened to that workload she couldn't
handle on her own?" Laura mused.

"Seems that she discovered a 'wonder boy' who
has settled in just marvelously, according to her,"
Brad drawled, as he mimicked Darlene.

"Is he a temporary employee?"

"I gathered he is more than an employee in several
ways. I think he has been added as a partner, plus
they hired the staff in his office."

Laura put her hand over his, her eyes soft with
compassion. "I'm sorry, Brad. I know this is a painful
time for you."

Brad agreed, dropped his head for a moment, then
looked up and held her eyes, earnestness burning in
his. "I'm a lot more comfortable here, but as you
suggested I need to go back to the real world and face
it. You've given me the courage and the motivation
to do just that."

"Motivation?" Laura questioned.

"Until I settle my old life, how can I go on with
the new?"

"New?"

"You. You are my life."

"That's because we're the only life you know right

now. When you recover, your wants and needs may change.''

"Nothing could change my wanting you. If it takes facing my past to enable my future, then I'm eager to get on with it, for I'm set on having you, Dr. Laura McBride." Determination fired his eyes.

Laura's face flushed at the raw emotion on his face and in his voice. She dropped her head, unwilling to let him see a response that offered encouragement.

"I'm sure they will all be relieved when you return," Laura murmured, changing the subject.

"Maybe," Brad responded, his voice unconvinced.

Laura wondered if this new turn of events posed a threat to Brad's aspirations. She shook her head. How could anyone pose a threat to the suave and charming Dr. Jeremiah once he regained his memory?

A sense of loss engulfed Laura as she considered how he had been when she had first met him. It was to that world he had set his mind to return. Would he revert to the man he was then? She shuddered in the warmth of the kitchen. Would the memory of last night, his confessions of devotion, be merely a passing interlude easily forgotten when his old world returned?

Although she tried, she could no longer deny the powerful emotions he stirred within her. Each time his dark eyes locked on hers, excitement charged through her. Just being in the room with him, the simple touch of his hand on hers, raced her heart. His intimate smile that seemed to say she was the only one in the world thrilled her as Mark's had never done. Emotions strong enough to cloud her resolve

threatened her rationality. Right now all she wanted
to do was to hide in his embrace, to brush away the
unruly lock that clung to his forehead, to comfort and
encourage him. More than anything she wanted to
hold him in her world. Here he was her Brad, the one
whose heart God had tendered, a man who had begun
a fragile and tentative search for the real meaning of
life, a meaning that reached beyond himself. Laura
groaned within, sorrowing that his leaving would
come before time had had a chance to solidify his
search and their relationship.

But which was the real Brad? The one she knew
and had begun to love, or the old Brad, focused, ambitious, charming and, perhaps, something else she
didn't want to consider?

Midmorning, the front desk paged Laura. She
picked up the phone in her office, to recognize the
well-modulated tones of Darlene on the other end.
She had called to find out the details of Brad's condition from Laura's point of view.

When Darlene hung up with a bright "Cheerio,"
she left a riot of questions agitating Laura's mind.
Laura wondered about her former suite mate and the
love she had professed for Brad. Her effusion over
their new staff doctor seemed to reach way beyond
the boundaries of professional interest.

Conflicting emotions assaulted Laura. A measure
of relief salved the guilt she had experienced since
Brad had first declared his love for her and denied his
affection for Darlene. Did she secretly hope Darlene's
love interest had shifted? And if it had, did that bode

problems for Brad's career future? His future and Darlene's relationship had appeared intricately entwined. Laura felt mixed feelings. While she would never want Brad to experience disappointment in his dreams and aspirations, she viewed his old world as a definite threat to her and any future relationship they might have. Yet would not true love stand the test of time and proving? If it wouldn't, then it was not love at all.

Laura slowly placed the telephone back in its cradle, as a sad smile curled one side of her mouth. One thing remained certain. Darlene had withdrawn the generous offer she had made to Laura in Louisville. She sighed and looked at the stark white walls surrounding her. Obviously destined to toil in these rural environs away from the excitement and financial success in the city, she steeled herself for the onslaught of disappointment she expected. Instead, only sweet relief permeated her heart.

Like a welcoming fresh breeze on a sultry day, an old proverb her mother had taught her wafted through her mind: "The steps of a wise man are ordained by God."

She smiled, believing.

The week passed quickly. Brad drove back to the Lovetts' house and followed David on his rounds at the hospital. Even Mark cooperated, putting his reticence toward this intruder at bay. With Brad's departure for Louisville imminent, the young doctor's affability returned and he insisted on helping any way he could.

One afternoon, he allowed Brad to observe in surgery, and afterward they went to the local eatery for a late meal. They had a lively discussion on the techniques Mark had used in surgery. Brad's eyes sparked with interest as he asked Mark questions about the unique procedures they employed with great success despite their limited equipment. Brad quizzed the younger doctor about the business setup of the hospital and his plans for the future.

When they were finished, Brad reached for the check and started to stand. Mark sat back in his chair and looked up. "Not so fast, Jeremiah. I'll let you buy my dinner, but I think we need to finish a conversation we had earlier."

Brad slowly returned to his seat, his brown eyes wary. "What's on your mind, Harrod?"

Mark asked, "Do you remember our conversation about Laura?"

"My short-term memory is fine, Mark."

"You indicated that I needed to make sure Laura was my girl," Mark continued, ignoring Brad's sarcasm.

"I haven't noticed you following my advice." Amusement flickered in Brad's eyes, then died as he encountered the determination in Mark's.

"You mistake patience for inaction," Mark drawled.

"Don't confuse lack of courage with patience," Jeremiah shot back.

"I haven't. You indicated that night that you couldn't afford to be interested in Laura. What changed?"

"I fell in love with her."

"What do you plan to do about it?"

"Move heaven and earth to have her."

"And what about that mysterious other life of yours? Earlier you said it stood in the way of any long-term commitment on your part. Do you think differently now, or is a longtime commitment not your definition of 'having her'?" Mark asked easily, while his eyes turned flinty.

"For such a congenial guy, you play rough, Harrod."

"No, just protecting someone dearer than life to me."

"Well, fight for her, man."

"You answer my question—I'll decide what I'll do about Laura."

"Will my answer influence your actions?"

"Yes."

"I love her with all my heart and soul. I can think of nothing more wonderful than spending the rest of my life with her by my side. That's why I'm going back. The future without her would be nothing but emptiness. Therefore, I must settle my past."

"I see. That's all I wanted to know."

"That's all?" Brad asked, confusion creasing his brow. "Are you giving up the fight?"

"In the famous old sea captain's vernacular, 'I have just begun to fight.' I had to know if you were sincere or toying with her. Makes a difference in my battle plan."

"Don't you want to know if she shares my feelings?" Brad grinned, admiration in his eyes.

"No, I'll find that out for myself. You see, I want you fully recovered, Jeremiah. I can't fight an unknown, nor do I want to compete with feelings of compassion, sympathy or latent maternal instincts disguising themselves as love."

"Now, just a minute, Harrod."

"You know as well as I do that sometimes a patient and doctor form emotional bonds, especially in a case of amnesia. She's been your whole world. Naturally, you'd form an attachment to her."

"She's more than an emotional crutch to me, if that's what you mean." Brad's eyes flashed anger.

"And then there is Laura," Mark cut in smoothly, ignoring Brad's retort. "A woman needs to be needed. You needed her. Being a doctor offers no protection from being a woman."

"You fool yourself if you think this is just a sick patient-doctor attachment. I love her. She is the essence of all my dreams, and if God so pleases, I want to spend my life making hers come true."

"I see." Mark's voice grew husky and his eyes softened with compassion as he looked at his handsome rival, his own feelings mirrored in the man's response. He added quietly, "Then may the best man win. The best man for Laura, that is." He reached across the table and offered his hand in friendship.

Brad shook Mark's hand warmly, a reluctant approval and a touch of fear in his eyes.

Mark's eyes met Brad's, and an impudent sparkle lit them as he reminded Brad, "Meanwhile, I'll have the home court advantage."

* * *

Brad's impending departure lay like a heavy weight on Laura's heart. Jonah watched and worried. Her appetite failed her and dark circles shadowed her eyes.

When Cassie McBride's car pulled into the long gravel driveway of the old farmhouse a sad smile twisted his mouth and he put on a kettle for tea. Jonah needed Cassie. He enjoyed her company, but it was her calm wisdom that he coveted now.

Jonah poured two cups of tea into the familiar old blue-willow cups and sat down across the table from her. Then his craggy brows drew together and he fastened his sharp blue eyes on her. "Cassie, you're a sight for these old eyes. I've been needing to talk to you."

Alarmed, Cassie set down her cup and stared into his eyes. "Why, Jonah, what's the matter?"

"Have you noticed our girl lately?"

"Haven't seen much of her in the past couple of weeks. Why?" Cassie drew in a quick breath.

"She appears tired and drawn. Hardly eats and she won't talk to me."

"You think she's worried about something?"

"It's more than worry—it's eating her alive." The old man leaned forward and looked Cassie in the eye. She dropped her head. "You know what's going on with her, now don't you?"

"I understand something of what she's going through," Cassie admitted.

"She talked to you?"

"Yes, two weeks ago."

"Then you can help her," Jonah stated, expelling a relieved sigh as he slumped back in his chair.

Cassie picked up her cup with both hands and studied the bottom of her tea before replying. Then she said softly, "No, Jonah, I can't help my daughter."

"If you can't, then who can?" the silver-haired old man demanded, frustration dancing in his keen blue eyes.

"No one. She's traveling the lonely road of decision. She's being torn between right and wrong, emotions and common sense."

Jonah replied, "Just what is bothering her, if I'm not intruding?"

Cassie laughed, a melodious laugh that eased the tension. "Just watch, Jonah. Your eyes will tell you."

The old man took his daughter-in-law's hand and shook his head. "I was afraid that was it. I kept denying it, mostly 'cause I feel guilty about insisting on his coming here."

"You're not responsible for the affairs of her heart. I believe that it is God who puts people in our path. Brad Jeremiah is not here by accident." Cassie placed a comforting hand on his gnarled ones.

"Surely you don't think he's right for our Laura!" Jonah exclaimed.

Cassie responded, patting his hand with affection, "I didn't say that. However, I wouldn't deny the possibility, either."

Jonah roared, "Sakes alive, Cassie, that young man, as congenial as he is, doesn't have a clue about God. They don't share the same faith. You know a relationship hasn't got a chance without God's superglue, so to speak."

Cassie took in a deep breath and let it out slowly.

"I am aware of that. But I also remember something else."

Jonah quizzed her with his eyes.

"God has a way of changing people. I should know. It was because I loved your son that I found God. This is Laura's chance to grow stronger by her choices. I believe that if her resolution remains firm, the opportunity for God to reach Brad will be greater."

"And if she doesn't?"

"She stands a chance to ruin two lives. Happiness never comes from compromising principle. Laura's faith is the very foundation of her life. If she and her mate don't share that, they will have no foundation on which to build a marriage."

"How can you be so calm?" Jonah declared, impatience in his voice.

"Calm? I'm not calm. I hurt because she hurts. I wish I could take her pain for her, walk the valley of indecision with her and make her decision for her, but I can't. I just know that in the end her decision will be the right one. And then she will emerge the woman God has intended her to become—with or without Brad Jeremiah. I leave that in God's hands."

Jonah looked long and hard at this daughter-in-law, whom he could not have loved more if she had been the seed from his own body. He raised her slender, expressive hand to his lips and replied, "How gracious God has been to me in giving me Anna, David and you. How could I doubt He would do any less for our precious Laura?"

Chapter Twelve

Brad collapsed on the old chintz sofa, his long legs stretched out in front of him. He burrowed his head in the inviting softness of the tall cushioned back and sniffed the pleasant aroma of supper, which wafted in from the kitchen. Closing his eyes, he placed one hand over them; a deep sigh issued from his lips.

Laura watched, hidden from his sight by the kitchen door. Her smile turned to a frown as she noted the lines of fatigue around his eyes. "Did the day go as badly as that?"

He jerked up his head and when his eyes encountered hers, they glowed with dancing fire. "Nothing of the sort. It was a good day. But then, every time I go with your dad, I learn something new."

"And what did the older doctor teach the younger doctor today?"

"No new techniques."

"Then what did you learn, Dr. Jeremiah?" She smiled as she moved toward him.

"Whatever it is that he has, I want."

"Your skill is equal to his, Brad."

"Maybe so, maybe not, but that's not what I mean."

Laura's brow furrowed as she sat down beside him. He sat up and moved to the corner, pulling her after him. He slipped his arm down the back of the seat around her and she nestled into the curve of his shoulders, then looked up into his face, a question in her eyes.

Before she could speak, Brad captured her lips with his. With a gentle tenderness his kiss expressed what was in his heart that seemed too inadequate for words. When he released her, Laura stared up into his warm brown eyes, a softness in them she'd never seen before. Then a mist clouded her vision and threatened to spill over, ruining the moment.

With a trembling finger she traced his lips, then asked, her voice husky, "Something has happened here. Care to tell me about it?"

"Over these past weeks, watching and listening to your dad made me see something about myself that I refused to consider."

"What?" Laura inquired, her heart pounding.

"My amnesia is not the source of my discontent."

Hope fired Laura's eyes. "It's not?"

"No, and rediscovering who I am won't bring contentment."

"And you've discovered what will?"

"I think so. Your dad told me that contentment

came as a result of knowing God and understanding who He made us to be.''

Laura nodded, afraid to speak. Encouragement in her eyes, she leaned in to him, and he took her hand and turned his head away, gazing into the distance, as if searching for the right words.

"I realized that I wanted to know Him, too," he whispered, perspiration beading his forehead.

"Because of me, Brad?" A shadow of doubt crossed her face.

"No, because of me. I had a void I needed filled, Laura." Now he looked her in the face, his eyes eager, pressing to convince her of the truth.

"'Had'?" Her heart fluttered; she scarcely believed her ears.

"Yes, had. Your dad explained how I could know Him and let Him fill that emptiness that plagued me."

"And what did you do?"

Brad grinned, dropped his head sheepishly. "I admitted my need and invited His Son into my life."

"Do you know what that means?"

"That I can know God through His Son, Jesus Christ, and He has the right to direct my life. To tell the truth, that's why it took me so long. A man has a hard time giving up control of own destiny. But as I watched your dad and Jonah day after day, I had to have what they had, whatever the cost."

"What?"

"Purpose and direction."

"Suppose God takes you in a direction you wouldn't choose?"

"I'm ready to follow," Brad said quietly as he took her hand in his.

Laura searched his eyes, then clutched his hand, acknowledging the sincerity that stared back at her. She couldn't trust her voice to speak; her heart was too full.

Brad delayed his return to Louisville, reluctant to pull himself from the place where he had found joy and contentment. Each day brought new discoveries. He dogged David's footsteps with questions and insisted on going on every journey David made. Gone was the veiled cynicism that always lurked under the surface. In exchange came an openness, an almost boyish eagerness for the day. His memory still sat submerged somewhere in the backwaters of his mind, refusing to surface, but he refused to let it trouble him.

Dr. Mark Harrod watched Brad's renaissance with mixed emotions. He rejoiced in Brad's new faith, while his heart ached; he realized this event put Laura further from his reach. Late one afternoon, Mark tarried at the nurses' station before making his last visit on his evening rounds. As he stared off into space, his only thoughts were of the dismal, lonely apartment that awaited him. And suddenly the years stretched before him in an empty blur, without Laura to inhabit them.

A pleasant voice with a clipped British accent spoke his name and he turned to look into a pair of expressive green eyes fringed with thick dark lashes that curled upward.

"What did you say, Gretchen?"

"A penny for your thoughts, Doctor."

Her smile was sweet; her hair framed a small oval face with pert nose, and a faint hint of lavender permeated the air around him as she leaned nearer. He stared at her a long minute before answering, his thoughts rioting as her beauty invaded his bleak moment. "They aren't worth that much," Mark replied, shaking his head sadly.

"Oh, come on, Dr. Mark. I can't remember you ever looking so glum. 'Tis a fine fall evening with just a hint of chill in the air. Surely you can think of something to cheer you up."

A reluctant smile crossed Mark's face. "Just forgot to count my blessings, I guess."

"We each have moments when our worries shadow all the good in our lives. I'm thinking that a good shepherd's pie would be cheering you up."

"Now, Gretchen, where would I be getting a shepherd's pie, whatever that is?" He grinned, suddenly responding to the warmth in her eyes.

"I just happen to have one prepared to go in the oven when I get home. It's much too big for me alone. Would you be interested in discovering the joys of a shepherd's pie?"

Mark's grin broadened, a cheerful glimmer returning to his dark eyes. "Sounds intriguing. What can I bring?"

"Just a hungry stomach and a soul that needs cheering. I think I can handle both just fine," she remarked with a grin, then turned on her heel to answer a patient's light. "See you at seven."

Laura drove the short distance between hospital and home, scarcely noticing the golden rays of late-afternoon sun as they bounced off the maple trees, which were just beginning to show their fall colors. She kept wondering how much longer Darlene would be content to let Brad stay away from his duties in Louisville. Every time the telephone rang in the evening she held her breath, afraid this would be the call that would separate them.

She opened the door and stepped into the shadows of the living room, and heard his smooth baritone singing in the kitchen. She smiled. He must be cooking tonight—or more likely grilling lamb chops, which were his specialty.

She pushed open the kitchen door and paused to stare at his back. She gazed at him from the top of his head to the soles of his shoes, and suddenly her eyes misted. He became more dear to her each day; what would she do when he went away? And what would happen when he regained his memory? Would she still be a vital part of his life? Or would his affection return to Darlene? She shuddered in the warm kitchen just as he turned.

A smile lit up his face as he spotted her across the room. "Hello, beautiful. I didn't hear you come in."

"Too busy with your culinary pursuits, were you, Dr. Jeremiah? I guess if doctoring becomes a bore, you can always be a chef."

He laughed. "That's an idea. We could call it 'Brad and Jonah's Diner.' Couldn't make it go without my buddy."

Laura looked up into his eyes. "You and Jonah really have hit it off."

The teasing lights in Brad's eyes grew serious. "He's like the father I never knew. And it's not just your granddad. Your whole family has taken me in, accepted me. They know nothing about me. Yet they extended warmth and affection without any merit on my part. It humbles me."

"I'm glad you like my folk, Brad," she answered, her voice husky with emotion.

"Like?" he asked, then chuckled. "The word doesn't begin to express my feelings. As for you, young lady..."

She grinned an impudent grin at him, daring him to speak his mind, "Yes, as for me..."

"It will take the rest of my life to adequately express the love I have for you."

Laura's smile broadened and her eyes glistened. "Whew, that's a relief. I thought you loved me for my family."

His hands went around her small waist and he lifted her up and whirled her around, then captured her lips in a gentle kiss as he slowly let her down. Her toes touched the floor; she leaned in toward him and slid both arms around his neck, her hands pressing his dark head to her. What had begun gently and tenderly suddenly ignited a flame that left them breathless.

When Brad pulled up his head from hers, his eyes were dark, glowing coals, and he whispered, "It's fortunate that you are in a protected environment, or I would have a difficult time ensuring my good conduct, Dr. McBride."

Laura stepped back, shaken at the volatility of their emotions, and attempted to make light of the moment. "I guess it's more than just my family that attracts you?"

Brad held her eyes as a wicked smile turned up one corner of his mouth and he agreed mildly, "You could say that, I reckon."

Laura's cheeks flamed and she dropped her head, unwilling for him to see the emotions that racked her soul.

He placed his hand under her chin and lifted it, forcing her to look at him. "What do you propose that I do about this 'attraction'?"

Held tightly in the grasp of his hand, she could not avoid his probing eyes. "I don't know. What do you want to do about it?"

"Throw you up on my white steed and whisk you through the forest away to my castle."

She laughed, despite her emotions, and responded, "That won't do. You have no horse and, as far as I know, no castle back in the forest."

"A mere technicality."

"You haven't considered the most important obstacle."

"And that might be, fair lady?"

"I don't belong to you," she reminded him, the smile fading from her face.

Pain touched his eyes before he gathered her into his embrace and murmured into her hair, "Oh, you belong to me. You've been mine since the first day your beautiful eyes saw the light of this world. I was just late finding you. God meant you for me. Someday soon I will make my claim. We'll say our vows and all that you are will be in my keeping until I draw my last breath. My heart, body and soul yearn for that moment.''

''Oh, Brad.'' Laura shuddered, then lifted her face up to his to receive his kiss.

What had burned with dangerous passion a few moments before now gentled with the promise of commitment. Their lips met, sealing the hope of a glorious tomorrow when they would be free to share all that love promised.

Still holding Laura in his embrace, Brad spoke. ''What hinders us now, Laura?''

''Only what lies buried in your memory, Brad.''

''I've thought it over. I don't want to return to Louisville. I want to stay here and work with your father. To carry on in his stead if need be.''

''Brad?'' She looked up into his face, scarcely believing what she heard.

''And throw away your promising career?''

''Not throw away. Reinvest it. I have no desire to return to Louisville.''

''But you must.''

''Why must I? I don't need any remembrance of past successes or failures, ambitions or disappointments. I'm free to carry on the work and I enjoy it. I found a place where I belong.''

''But, Brad, how can you know you belong here until you're sure you don't belong where you were? Unless you go back to face your past, we can't have a present or a future,'' Laura said, wresting herself from his grasp.

"How could I ever want anything more than sharing this world with you?"

"You aren't free to make that choice until you find out you have the right to choose," Laura insisted.

"What reason could possible hinder my choosing you and a life here in these mountains?"

Suddenly, the resonate door chimes rang through the house. Brad looked questioningly at Laura, who shrugged. "If it's Harrod, he's picked a good night to intrude. We've got plenty of food."

"Brad!" Laura chastised.

"Oh, all right, go let him in. I just don't like sharing my girl."

Laura opened the door with a broad smile and Mark's name on her lips, where it hung in the air, unspoken. A tall, slender woman with glistening dark hair and large black eyes fringed with long thick lashes stood framed in the doorway. Her full scarlet mouth slashed a face of perfect proportions and flawless skin. Heavy gold chains adorned one arm, while a gold watch encrusted with diamonds encircled the opposite shapely wrist. Her expensive, deep-green jersey dress draped a perfect figure, the scoop neckline revealing a large emerald pendent.

"I'm looking for Dr. Brad Jeremiah," she stated brusquely, scrutinizing Laura from head to toe, before giving a slight shrug as if to dismiss her. Then she smiled, a cold, tight smile. "Is he here?"

"Yes, he is. I'll get him for you." Laura stepped back and motioned her inside.

Brad called from the kitchen, "Laura, tell Mark his

timing is perfect and is he in for a treat. Never mind, I'll tell him myself.''

Brad pushed open the kitchen door, wiping his hands on the towel that he had draped around his waist. He looked up with a welcoming smile on his lips and straight into the two black eyes that rested on him.

All the color drained from Brad's face and he stood frozen to the parlor floor. "Mona," he whispered, while raw emotion fired his eyes.

One look told Laura that all his forgotten yesterdays had returned in one cataclysmic moment. And she felt sick.

Mona glided across the old pine floor toward Brad with the sensuous grace of a panther, her eyes devouring him. "My, my, it seems you've recovered quite nicely. Darling, you never looked better.''

She stepped closer, her perfume haunting the air. Running her hands up Brad's arms to his broad muscular shoulders, where they lingered, then moved slowly in a caressing sweep behind his neck, she planted her scarlet mouth on his. After what seemed an eternity to Laura, Mona pulled back her head and smiled triumphantly into Brad's eyes, her voice low and sultry.

"Well, Dr. Jeremiah, welcome home.''

Laura cleared her throat. "I'll leave you two alone. You seem to have a lot of catching up to do. If you need me, Brad, I'll be upstairs.''

With Mona still wrapped around him, Brad jerked his head toward her. Disbelief contorting his face, his dark eyes tortured coals, he murmured, "Oh, excuse me, Laura, this is..."

"Yes, Mona, I gathered that. Now, if you will excuse me," Laura said through tight lips, fighting to control her emotions lest Brad and Mona see the pain that wrenched her.

Mona slid one arm down Brad's back and held on to him possessively as she turned to Laura, dismissing her. "Thank you, we do have a lot to discuss. Don't we, darling?"

Laura left the room with as much dignity as she could muster, then ran up the stairs to her room, her breath coming in gasps, tears stinging her eyes. When she reached the sanctity of her room, they spilled over and silent sobs racked her body, the image of Brad with Mona in his arms seared into her memory.

Downstairs, Brad stood paralyzed in the lengthening shadows in the old familiar parlor. Like a film in slow motion, he looked at each piece of furniture that had become dear to him, smelled the aroma of baking bread wafting from the kitchen, as the deepest sense of mourning filled his soul.

Mona spoke his name, and like a bolt of lightning, he came to himself. After placing his hands roughly on her shoulders, he pushed her away from him. "You know better than that Mona."

"What's the matter? That little doctor gal your new love?"

"That's none of your affair, Mona. What is relevant is that you are a married woman."

"Correction, an unhappily married woman."

"If I remember rightly, that was your decision."

"We all make mistakes."

"But some are irreversible."

"I don't want to reverse mine, just mitigate it. And you're just the one to help me," Mona crooned.

"Not me. You had your chance and made your choice when you chose power, prestige and wealth over love."

"Darling, I didn't do it just for me."

"Really?"

"Oh, get that sanctimonious look off your face. You are just as ambitious as I am."

"Not enough to use people."

Mona threw back her head and laughed, a tinkling sound that bounced off the walls and floors. "You used me to get where you are. If it wasn't for me, you'd still be what you were when I first saw you— a trauma surgeon at a hospital, on constant call, with a pauper's pay."

"I'd like to think my skill and reputation had something to do with my success."

"Oh, Brad, I have a lot bigger plans for you. Why do you think I married Larry?"

"Other than his money and influence, why did you marry him?"

"For you. I saw a chance to further your career."

"That's a new twist. I thought you were supposed to marry for love. As I remember that was all I had to offer you."

"It is more pleasant if you love the person you marry, but some things outweigh emotions."

"Like wealth and position."

"Larry is one of the most powerful men in Washington. He has had the ear of the presidents for a decade.''

"I'm sure I couldn't care less what your husband does. All that matters to me is that he is your husband and you have no business here.''

"That's not what you thought the day your plane crashed.''

"What matters is what I think today. You are a married woman. Whatever was between us before is over, closed, no exceptions. So if you will find your way back the same way you came, we'll forget this ever happened.''

Anger glittered in Mona's eyes. "Not so fast. You can't deny how much you love me. I remember how you begged me to marry you right up to the night before my wedding. You were distraught.''

"I'm not distraught now, Mona, and what I felt for you was not love.''

She laughed again, this time derisively. "You must still have amnesia if you don't remember what we had.''

"I vividly remember and it wasn't love.''

"No?'' She arched an eyebrow.

"I've learned the difference between lust and love. All I had for you was a physical craving.''

"Had?'' She smiled seductively.

"Had,'' he answered firmly, his eyes holding hers. "It's over.''

"Does Goldilocks have anything to do with your newly found discernment?'' Mona asked, nodding toward the stairs.

"As a matter of fact, she has everything to do with it."

"What a pity. The plans I have for you don't include her."

"Any plans you have for me are not relevant."

"You're mistaken, Brad." Her thin voice took on a hard edge. "I'm in a position to propel you to career heights you've never dreamed of. I wasn't joking when I said I married Larry for you. Of course I wanted what he had to offer me, but I saw what he could do for both of us." A sly smile parted her lips and she added quietly, "The office of Surgeon General is not out of the question."

"You are crazy." Brad shook his head.

She moved toward him, then lifted her well-manicured hand to his face and patted his cheek. "Just crazy for you, darling."

Brad shuddered at her touch as memories filled his mind. Suddenly, revulsion filled his mouth, tasting like gall. "Then you'll just have to get over it. I'm no longer available."

Anger sparked in her eyes and she spoke, determination in her voice. "You will always be available to me."

Incredulity widened Brad's eyes, and he clamped his jaws, then responded, "I'm not interested in anything you have to offer, Mona. Now, leave."

"Did your memory not remind you of why you were coming to me?"

Brad's dark eyes darted to and fro; something in the back of his mind bubbled but refused to surface.

Then it found escape, disgust contorting his features, his mouth twisting in a grimace.

A triumphant smile parted Mona's cold, perfect face. "You remember," she whispered.

He dropped to the sofa, his head in his hands. A quiet groan of agony tore through the silence in the room, silence broken only by the ticking of the stately grandfather clock.

Chapter Thirteen

Laura splashed water on her face and took one last look in the mirror, then raised a resolute chin. "Lady, if you think you can walk into my home and steal my happiness, you better think again."

She started toward her bedroom door, determined to return to the parlor, when a gentle knock sounded. She stopped midstride, her heart in her throat. "Yes?"

"It's Brad. May I come in?"

"Of course. The door's not locked." She backed away, sensing the anguish in his voice.

Even then she was not prepared for his agonized appearance. His handsome face appeared haggard and old. The color that had drained away at the sight of Mona had not returned, and his eyes had a dull, resolved look.

Laura recognized defeat in his countenance and

knew she had lost the battle before she had begun to fight.

A smile trembled on her lips, then failed, and she motioned to the alcove, where the two old comfortable chairs sat looking out over the valley and the mountains beyond.

"No, thank you, I haven't time. Mona is waiting to take me back to Louisville."

"Tonight?" Her voice rose; panic bubbled inside her. So soon? Would she get no time alone with him? Time to persuade him?

"Yes, the sooner the better."

"I see," she answered, denying the blindness that cloaked her understanding.

"No, you could hardly see."

"You want to clear up some loose ends and return?"

"No, Laura. This is goodbye."

"Goodbye?" For a moment her panic surfaced and her heart raced; then she pushed it back, refusing to let it control her actions.

"I'm afraid so," he confirmed.

"What about us, our plans, the excitement of working here, the purpose and contentment you talked about?"

"I'm afraid that was little more than make-believe." With a sad sigh, he continued, still making no sense to Laura. "As Mark warned me earlier, my sojourn here was only a beautiful escape."

Laura flinched as if he had slapped her. "All of it? Was I make-believe, too? Or were you just amusing yourself with me?"

"Of course not, but you have to understand." His eyes pleaded for her comprehension. "That moment in the parlor when my memory returned, bringing my old life with it, I knew the old and the new were incompatible," he murmured as he shook his head, his broad shoulders sagging.

"What do you want, Brad? The old or the new?" she asked, afraid to hear his answer, yet desperate to know.

"What I want is not the issue. It seems that my past choices dictate my future." Resignation set his face in a lifeless mask.

"What choices, Brad? Surely you have the freedom to change those choices. You're not the same man you were."

"The Brad you knew was only an illusion, Laura. I am tied irrevocably to the old Brad. Decisions made that can't be recalled determine the course my life will take."

"And I have no place in that life?"

Sadness haunted his eyes and he shook his head. "You wouldn't be happy."

"If you were there, I would be," she argued.

"Not for a moment. You wouldn't fit into my world."

"It doesn't have to be your world anymore."

"I'm bound to it, Laura."

"Then take me with you," she begged, a sudden fear for his future overriding her pride.

"You are too innocent and pure for my world. It would only defile you and I couldn't bear that."

"Defile? What horrible choices have bound you?

Don't return. Not for my sake but for yours," she pleaded, even while she knew his mind was closed.

"That's the only place I'm fit for," he snarled, his mouth a thin line of disgust.

"Mona convinced you of that?"

"No, my own memories."

"You can start afresh. God forgives and restores."

"The cost of forgiveness is too great."

Laura gasped; fear gripped her heart. "What cost?"

"My future, everything I ever wanted in life."

"Your career?"

"Yes."

"What about me?"

"Either way I've lost you."

"How can you say that? I love you. Nothing you've done could make me stop loving you."

"Won't you believe that I love you too much to stay or to take you with me?"

"No, because real love doesn't run away." She shook her head vigorously, her eyes imploring.

"But it does protect. I refuse to let you suffer the consequences of my choices." Brad clenched his jaw, his eyes dulled with pain.

He took a step toward her and placed his hand beneath her chin, lifting it so her eyes met his. "Laura, the memory of you will be the one bright and shining moment of my life, a reminder of what my life could have been."

Brad placed a tender kiss on her lips. Then he was gone.

* * *

For the next two weeks Laura attended her duties with the vitality of a robot. Every action was methodical and detached. Her family noticed, but only Jonah questioned. He could get very little out of her other than her official explanation: "Brad's memory had returned and so had he." She gave no reason, no further explanation, and finally even Jonah retreated in the face of her misery.

Dr. Mark Harrod watched and waited. At every opportunity, he tried to revive the old lively comradeship he and Laura had enjoyed before Dr. Brad Jeremiah had invaded their lives. But the Laura he knew had exited when Brad walked out of her life.

Heartache devoured her youth, consuming her dreams. She dared not consider her future. Safety rested in absorption in day-to-day routine. When Mark invited her out for a pizza and movie, she looked at him as if he'd invited her to the moon, then she declined.

As the days of isolation drifted into weeks, Mark turned more and more to the enchanting company of Gretchen. In her he found release and a kindred spirit. They were careful to keep their dates quiet, not wanting to feed the gossip mill at the hospital with romantic speculation. For what they enjoyed was not romance but a deepening friendship.

One late afternoon Laura stopped in the village to pick up a few groceries and the evening paper for Jonah. As she stood in line, she idly turned the pages, reading without absorbing what she read. Suddenly, a picture and caption riveted her attention.

A handsome giant with dark hair and brooding eyes

looked out from the paper. Beneath the picture she read about the very popular Dr. Brad Jeremiah, who had recently returned to his local practice after recovering from injuries when his plane crashed. A tall man with silver hair stood on one side of him, while on the other a slender dark-haired beauty posed with one possessive hand on his arm. There was no doubt about her identity—Mona, staking her claim for the world to see. But who was the man with them?

She sucked in her breath, holding it, as she read the names: Senator John Durham and his wife, Mona. Laura groaned; the barrier she had placed around her heart came tumbling down. "Oh, no, Brad. Not a married woman. You can't. How can she possibly make you?"

Laura managed to pay for her purchases, then stumbled to her car, tears blinding her. She started the engine and roared out of the parking lot, the landscape a blur. She drove for miles, not willing to go home and face Jonah. To face him would be to answer questions that would shatter his belief in Brad. Yet the pain she had sealed inside her now reached a crescendo that demanded release. Suddenly, she made a U-turn, to a chorus of irritated horns, and sped toward Mark Harrod's small bleak apartment to seek solace from the gentle man who had always been there for her when she needed him.

When Mark opened his door, the wide expectant smile on his face faded. He invited her in, and suddenly, the dam broke and all the suppressed pain and agony poured out. Mark gathered Laura into his arms and she sobbed on his shoulder, soaking his shirt.

When finally the sobs subsided, he asked, "Do you want to tell me about it?"

Between gulps of air, she showed him the picture and told him the story.

Laura failed to see the pain in Mark's eyes as she described her love for Brad, nor did she notice him clamp his jaws in anger. All she recognized was the sweet release of being able to share her heartache with someone who cared.

Afterward she looked up, her swollen red-rimmed eyes large and questioning. She felt as if she had found a haven from the storm. Then her anguish boiled over again. "Did he really love me? Or was I a pleasant diversion while he recuperated?"

"As angry as I feel for his hurting you, I know he loved you."

"How?"

"I asked him about his intentions."

"And what did he say?"

"That he wanted to spend the rest of his life with you, that nothing could ever change that."

Tears filled Laura's eyes again, threatening to spill out. "When?"

"The night the two of us went out to dinner after work."

"I can't believe you two discussed me like that," she objected. "But why?"

"I wanted to make sure he wouldn't harm you. Seems I failed," he commented dryly.

"Oh, Mark, you are precious. Just like a big brother protecting my honor." She smiled through her tears, touched by Mark's concern.

"No, Laura, not like a big brother," he corrected, holding her gaze.

Abruptly turning from her, he walked over to his small compact desk and rummaged through the drawer until he found a clean white handkerchief. He handed it to her and she blew her nose.

A tremulous smile fought with her emotions and she looked at him, stuttering, "Thank—thank you, Mark. For always being here when I need you."

He patted her hand gently. "That's what friends are for."

"I don't know what I expected you to do."

"Listen, that's all. I don't have any answers. But you needed to release this pain. Your emotions have been like a boil that has needed lancing. Tonight you lanced it. Perhaps now the healing can begin."

"How will I ever recover? You can't imagine how it feels, Mark, to love someone so deeply and lose him."

Mark winced, but Laura, wrapped in her own misery, never noticed the pain in his eyes. "Time is a great healer, Laura. First you come out of the shock, then you hurt, then you release it and then you heal. Tonight the healing begins."

"Mark, how would you know?" she asked.

He tweaked her chin and tried to smile, the merry lights in his eyes extinguished. "I'm not just a doctor, Laura. I'm a man, too."

"How thoughtless of me to bring my heartache to you."

"Don't worry about me, kitten. It was more painful just watching you suffer."

"What should I do about this sad state of affairs, Mark?" she asked.

"What do you want to do?"

"I want to go chasing after him to Louisville and drag him back here."

Mark winced anew, then chuckled. "I don't think that would be the wisest course of action."

"Because he has made it clear that he doesn't want me?"

"No, because he has made it clear that he doesn't want you involved. There's a big difference."

"What could be so terrible that he abandoned our love and his plans?"

"We may never know."

"No matter what he has done, he needs to face it."

"Maybe he will."

"No, he said the cost would be too great."

"He's discounting the misery he faces if he doesn't address it. I don't know what his problem is, but he does have a conscience to deal with."

"Sometimes ambition will sear it. I think that Mona reminded him of what he had before the accident and in the final analysis he couldn't let it go. He decided that I didn't fit into his plans or Mona's."

"It will do you no good to hash and rehash questions that have no answers."

"Then where do I begin?"

"Have you considered trusting God for the outcome?" Mark's soft voice gently suggested.

Laura grimaced and dropped her head, "Trust? How can I, when I feel so abandoned?"

"By God or Brad?" Mark reached for her hands,

clasping them in his, pain and understanding darkening his ebony eyes.

"Both." Laura murmured, shame flushing her face.

Mark placed a finger under her chin, lifting it, forcing her to meet his eyes. "A natural reaction when faith conflicts with feelings."

"I'm so ashamed. I thought my faith was so strong, then here I am floundering as if I had none." She twisted away from him and stood up.

"On the other side of this struggle it will be stronger." Mark encouraged.

"How could anything good come from these circumstances?" Laura wailed, standing above him, her jaws clenched.

"When you are able to quit demanding answers and acknowledge that He's God and, whatever the outcome, He has your best interests at heart," Mark responded, his gaze holding hers.

"But I'm afraid, Mark," she admitted.

"Of what Laura?" Mark probed, forcing her to search her heart.

"That what God wants and what I want may not be the same." She collapsed on the sofa beside him, the unwilling confession draining the little strength she had left.

A sad and knowing smile parted Mark's lips, not quite reaching his eyes, "Then that's where you begin, my sweet."

Laura reached out and grabbed Mark's hand. Looking up into his face, her wide blue eyes pled, as her voice whispered, "Help me, Mark."

Mark leaned over and lifted her chin with one hand

then placed a gentle kiss on her forehead and whispered, "Whatever it takes, my little one."

And for the first time in weeks, Laura felt comforted.

The last leaves of a golden fall clung stubbornly to the red oak trees outside the hospital. Brown and dry, they waited for the rebirth of spring to dislodge them. A brisk November wind scraped the branches against the brick wall, rustling the leaves with a desolate sound that matched the gray sky. The crisp air, with the smells of cinnamon and apples, wood smoke and cider, took on an early winter's bite and Laura pulled her scarlet jacket close around her body and hunched into the wind, ducking her head.

Although the furrows in her brow had eased, the sparkle in her eyes had yet to return. She gave herself totally to her work, and some days several hours would pass without thoughts of Brad haunting her memory. Then, turning in the hall or sitting on her sofa, the image of his dark good looks would rise like a specter.

Laura curled up by the fire as a cold, lonely November wind howled outside. Holding a new novel in her hands, she fought to keep her mind on the story and off her heartache. She grimaced when the telephone rang, fearing it was the hospital and dreading to go back out into the cold wind.

"Dr. McBride here," she answered crisply.

"Well, Dr. McBride, haven't talked to you in a long while," Darlene announced cheerily.

The past came flooding in, draining the color from Laura's face. Her voice was thin as she politely responded, "Hello, Darlene, what a surprise to hear from you."

"Not as surprised as you're going to be, Laura. I'm getting married." Her former suite mate's voice fairly rang with excitement.

Laura's heart jumped a beat and for a moment her voice failed to respond, then she murmured, "When is the big day?"

"The Friday after Thanksgiving, in the university chapel. I'm calling to ask you to serve as my maid of honor."

Laura's pale face flushed and her heart pounded as she stammered, "I—I don't think I can make it, Darlene."

"Why not, Laura?"

"I'll probably be on duty that weekend."

"Find someone to cover for you while you're here. This is a special event," she persisted.

"Yes, special, but I can't m-make it," she stuttered.

"But, Laura, you're the only one I want to be my maid of honor."

"Why?"

"Because it would mean so much to me for you to share in my happiness. Besides, you'll make a beautiful bridesmaid," Darlene rattled on, scarcely taking a breath.

"It's out of the question, but I do hope you and Brad will be very happy," Laura responded; her heart felt like heavy lead in her chest.

"Brad?" Darlene asked, finally pausing. "You thought I was marrying Brad?"

"Aren't you? You were engaged to him."

"That's old history now. I'm marrying Dr. Ted Arnez, the new partner who came when Brad was injured. And I'm so happy."

"How can that be?" Laura questioned, curiosity compelling her to ask. "I thought you loved Brad."

"I thought I did, but I found out what I felt for him wasn't love."

"Not love?" Laura's interest was riveted; she felt as if her heart had stopped.

"It was attraction—he is a handsome and charming man, you know."

"I noticed," Laura murmured into the phone, the corner of her mouth drooping.

"Also, I think it was the thrill of conquest. All the women had set their caps for him and when he chose me, the former ugly duckling, I was flattered into believing it was love. His accident gave me a lot of time to sort out my feelings. I realized that not once had he told me he loved me, nor had I him. And then there was always Mona lurking in the background."

"Yes, there's Mona," Laura agreed.

"Anyway, when I met Ted I realized what love was for the first time in my life."

The phone silence between them grew as Laura fought conflicting emotions that raged through her.

Finally Darlene asked, "Laura, are you still there?"

"Yes, Darlene, you just took me by surprise."

Darlene's laugh tinkled over the wires, and Laura

visualized her friend's eyes large and luminous with happiness. Envy shot through her, bringing a physical pain to her chest.

Darlene continued, "Love took me by surprise. I thought marriage would be a businesslike contract where two people shared common goals and purposes but lived independently. Now all I want to do is become the most intimate part of Ted's life. If I succeed in my practice, fine, but loving him and being his wife are the most important things in my life."

"He must be a fine man."

"He is. Not handsome and polished in the way Brad is, but he's real. And when those green eyes look at me, I feel like a queen. You would admire him, Laura. He has a strong set of values and has made some changes in our practice here."

"I'm surprised he has been able to do that," Laura murmured.

"He has had to move slowly because it has been a battle all the way with Mona."

"What does Mona have to do with your practice?" Laura asked, cold fingers gripping her heart.

"She sits in her father's stead on the board now. He has taken his new wife for a tour around the world and left all his business decisions to Mona."

"And Brad?"

"He keeps a low profile, but if the chips were down, I'm sure he would vote with Mona. After all, she's been his job security for too many years for him to abandon her now. She's not a nice person when she doesn't get her way."

"How has she been his job security?"

"She met him in the hospital emergency room when he was the trauma surgeon there. She liked what she saw and went after him. They were quite an item for a while, then she up and married this big shot from Washington and Brad suddenly was in private practice with her dad. You go figure."

"I've tried to," Laura said under her breath.

"What did you say, Laura?"

"Never mind. I was just trying to fit the pieces together."

"Oh, that's right. You've met Mona. When she came here steaming, I sent her to your house. I guess she got what she wants, but I'm not so sure about Brad."

"Why?"

"He looks terrible and he's been in an awful mood since he returned. Not at all his old, charming self."

"I saw his picture in the paper. Seemed pretty happy to me." Laura tried to keep her voice steady.

"That one with Mona?" Darlene asked.

"Yes," Laura answered tersely, lest her voice betray her.

"He has been making the social rounds with Mona and her distinguished hubby. Rather mysterious. But then, Brad was never easy to figure out. Anyway, I guess you're glad to get him out of your hair."

"Something like that," Laura said barely above a whisper, as pain real and physical racked her insides.

"Now then, enough about him. Won't you please be in my wedding?"

"I don't think so."

"Nonsense, I won't take no for an answer. I've already bought your dress."

Laura's temples pounded and she clasped and unclasped her hands. In the end she agreed because she couldn't disappoint a friend, even at great cost to her peace of mind.

Thanksgiving week arrived on a cold north wind. The sky hung low and gray, with the smell of snow in the air. Laura worked feverishly through Wednesday morning with an anxious eye to the weather.

About midmorning she looked up from her desk directly into the warm brown eyes of Mark Harrod. He lounged against her file cabinet with his arms crossed, an impudent grin on his face.

She gave him an absentminded smile, her mind absorbed in her work. "Hi, Mark, don't have time to chat. These records have to be finished before I leave at noon."

"That's what I came by about. What time are we leaving?"

"We?" she asked, her attention suddenly captured.

"Yes, we." He grinned. "I asked the boss if I could have a holiday, and although he looked harried at the thought of having his right hand away for four whole days, he gave his reluctant approval."

"Mark! What a wonderful idea!"

"Good. Your car or mine? On the second thought, I'll pick you up. We'll be safer in a four-wheel drive vehicle than that little spider you call a car."

She made a face at him. "Don't you know you'll hurt my feelings, attacking my pride and joy?"

"I'd risk that if I could persuade you to get a safer vehicle. You drive too fast. You act like the car is invisible the way you whip in and out of traffic." He shuddered.

Laura leaned back and laughed, the tension easing from her face. "I'm delighted you can go to Louisville, and I'll not even mind riding in your old clunker."

"She's not an old clunker. She's a mature masterpiece," Mark argued.

"Who's not an old clunker?" asked Gretchen as she entered the small office with a cup of coffee in her hand.

Laura laughed. "Gretchen, Mark is trying to convince me that his car is far superior to mine and therefore we should take it to Louisville."

"Louisville?" Gretchen inquired. She paused as she handed the cup in her hand to Laura.

"Thank you, I was needing a break. Yes, he's taking me to my friend's wedding," Laura explained as she took a gulp of the hot liquid and winced.

Gretchen turned to Mark, her eyes wide and questioning. "Are you, now? And how long would you be staying?" Her clipped accent was a little more prominent.

"That's right, Gretchen. Going to a wedding. But I'm not getting any ideas," he replied, as a message flashed between them.

"Now, that's a good thing I'll be agreeing with, Dr. Mark. Guard your heart. Weddings can make you vulnerable."

"Mark, vulnerable?" Laura queried with a puzzled smile.

"Maybe I'd better rephrase that. Weddings sometimes give us longings that can't be fulfilled."

"You've had those, too?" Mark asked.

Gretchen smiled and nodded. "Wouldn't we all be surprised if we could read the hearts and the minds of one another?"

Laura looked closely at the pretty nurse and noted a strange sadness in her. Then she remembered their conversation about Mark the week of Brad's plane crash. Did Mark realize that Gretchen's longing was for him? A shiver ran down her spine. Did love have to be like this? What a mixed-up world! Laura pining for Brad and Gretchen pining for Mark. And who did Mark want? She knew the answer and felt guilty that it comforted her.

The small chapel shimmered in the soft glow of a hundred candles. Laura squinted, scanning the compact room from the back. The organ began to play and a hush fell over the crowd packing the pews. Bejeweled women and distinguished men looked expectantly toward the center door and Laura stepped back beyond their view.

Her formfitting dress of blue silk turned her eyes to cobalt and emphasized the perfect proportions of her figure. The weight she had recently lost lent a new fragile quality to her beauty and accented her cheekbones. Her skin looked luminous in the candlelight; her hair fell softly around her shoulders. She picked up her bouquet of sweetheart roses and sniffed. Then frowned. Where was the fragrance? They only smelled of refrigeration.

The soloist finished and Laura breathed a sigh of relief. She had seen neither Brad nor Mona in the crowd and now it was her time to precede Darlene down the long center aisle.

Tears stung Laura's eyes as Darlene vowed her love and life to the young man whose shock of red hair and sprinkle of freckles on his nose made him appear an unlikely candidate for the chic lady doctor. But the adoration that fired his vivid green eyes as he received her pledge quickly put such a presumption to rest and envy struggled to have its way in Laura.

She handed Darlene the ring and stepped back, searching for Mark's comforting presence. Instead she found a dark head that towered above the others. The dark brooding eyes in his handsome, patrician face fixed on her. The months of separation had changed nothing. The sadness of his countenance, the yearning in his gaze, pronounced what his voice could not. And for an instant hope revived in her heart.

Laura scanned the faces of the people who swarmed into the reception hall, but Brad's was not among them. The hope that had ignited in the chapel died and an onslaught of pain deluged her. It seemed physical in its intensity. She shouldn't have come. Why would she open herself up for such suffering?

Darlene had said it was because she couldn't let a friend down. But standing in the church with Brad's eyes on her, she knew the real reason she had come. It wasn't for Darlene but for Laura; she'd hoped to see Brad, hoped that things would be magically all right. But they weren't and it was time for her to face the finality of his decision. Her head felt light and she called for Mark. He rushed to her side, as always her support in weakness. They made their excuses and left. The bride had yet to throw her bouquet, but Laura was in no mood to catch it.

Chapter Fourteen

He watched her from the shadows, his soul hungry for the touch of her. He knew that he should have left when he'd glimpsed her standing in the foyer, but he couldn't. Slipping in unnoticed, while her back was turned, he puzzled why Darlene had not told him she would be there.

Of course he'd seen very little of Darlene since his return. Fact is, he'd seen very few people except for the isolated social outings that Mona had coerced him into attending. He just did his job and went home to brood. Now and then he worried about when and what kind of demands Mona might make, but so far her husband had kept her too busy entertaining important people to think about running his life.

A mirthless chuckle rumbled in his throat, his eyes cold and hard in the semidarkness. Mona was in her element playing hostess to the high rollers. When she'd called, she bragged about her guest list and whispered it was all in her plan to ensure his future. Didn't she know, that without Laura he had no future? Without her, his life was but an empty shell.

He shivered remembering how he had told Laura that the price of forgiveness was too high. She thought he meant sacrificing his career. Losing his career was not what he dreaded; it was the look he would see in those glorious eyes if he told her the truth about his life. How could he bear watching the soft tender light of love in them turn hard; how could he stand her hating him, even as he despised himself? Yet had he not chosen the coward's way out? Without his telling her, she would never know the depths of his love. She must feel used, cheapened that she'd given her love to someone who treated it so lightly.

He grimaced and jealousy wrenched his gut when Mark Harrod took her arm and guided her through the crowd; her face turned very pale. She looked thin, vulnerable. She passed near enough that he smelled her perfume. Pain, dagger sharp, pierced his insides. Beneath his breath he groaned. He wanted to reach out and touch her, to feel her velvet skin against his fingertips.

She didn't see him; she had her head down and Mark spoke softly to her, then gathered her beneath his shoulder as they walked out the door together. And for a moment Brad hated Mark Harrod.

A cold blast of wind blew down the hall before the door slammed shut, bringing sanity to him, and he watched them through the window as they paused in the golden glow of the street lamp. Mark removed his jacket and tenderly wrapped it around her. She reached up and caressed his cheek.

Brad's breath came in short, ragged gasps. He could feel her touch and ached to be where Mark was, his arms holding her, his body protecting her from the elements of nature, from the dangers of the night. The yearning to feel her caress against his face seemed more than he could bear. He had lost that privilege before he possessed it. How could he allow her to walk away, out of his life, perhaps never to see her again? Yet how could he do anything else? What was different from when he had walked out on her? Had there been any resolution in his life that would spare her? Desperate to delay the inevitable, he slipped from the building and like a stealthy shadow followed them to their hotel.

Laura, craving time alone to sort out her battered emotions and to bury her dreams, had dismissed Mark and ordered a pot of hot chocolate and a sandwich from room service. She slipped out of her dress into a emerald green dressing gown and brushed her hair until it looked like a spun golden cloud. A knock interrupted her as she reached to remove her makeup.

"Room service," came the terse announcement, and she heard dishes clattering.

After taking money from her purse, she opened the door. The slight smile on her face froze as she whispered, "Brad."

Brad took the tray from the waiter, who watched the scene with interest. He searched her face before he asked, "May I come in?"

"Do you think that's wise?" she queried, giving the man a generous tip.

"No. But I have no choice."

Her laugh was cold. "I believe you said that the last time I saw you."

"I said all the wrong things and none of the right." He stood there in the doorway, filling it, his hat in his hand, his eyes pleading. "Please let me in."

She nodded and turned back into the room.

"Would you like a cup of hot chocolate?" she inquired, a cool civility replacing her usual warmth.

He looked at her, holding her eyes for a long moment, and then said, "All I want is to be near you."

Anger flashed in her eyes, and sarcasm laced her voice. "You've had a change of heart?"

He flushed, the memory of their last meeting vivid. "No. I've always felt this way about you, since that first night you walked into my apartment like some golden princess."

"Is that what you came to tell me?" she asked with an incredulous chuckle.

"No." He shook his head, and a sigh issued from him. "I no longer have the right. When I tell you why I came, you won't want me to love you," he replied with a sad sigh.

Laura sat down on the sofa and poured herself a cup of hot chocolate, making a big production of it in a futile effort to disguise the pain she was feeling. She curled her feet beneath her like a little girl and took the cup in both hands, sipping the mahogany beverage slowly and deliberately. Its warmth felt good to her chilled body. Studying her cup, she avoided his eyes as she replied, "All right, go ahead, sit down. Say whatever it is you need to say."

Brad sat on the opposite end of the sofa and placed his hat on the floor, then leaned toward her. "The night I left you, I was in a state of shock and was not thinking clearly."

"If you made a mistake, you could have called—or returned." Laura's voice faltered. She turned eyes on him filled with pain, matching the agony in his.

"I didn't make a mistake leaving," he explained, hesitant as he searched for the right words. "I made a mistake in not telling you the real reason I left."

"Then why now?"

"I had convinced myself it was best for you. But when I saw you tonight, I realized that I had chosen what was best for me. I couldn't go on without sharing the truth with you."

"If it won't change anything, why bother?" she asked, not convinced she wanted to hear what he wanted to tell her.

"Because I want you to go on with your life not believing I traded you for something or someone more important to me."

"Then why did you leave?"

"Because I was not worthy of you."

"What made you decide that?"

"Mona. Her arrival made me remember the final piece of the puzzle—where I was going the day my plane crashed. Until that question was answered, there could be no you and me. But once it was, I realized you wouldn't want me. That's what I couldn't bear."

Laura frowned, not understanding. "What?"

"For you to know the truth and despise me."

"So it was better for me to think you didn't want me? That you toyed with my love?"

"No, better for me. I took the selfish way out. That is, until I saw you. Then I knew I couldn't go on without setting things straight. The greatest part of my punishment will be to lose you, that I lost your love for what I am."

"And the lesser?" she probed.

"Losing my career."

She stared at him. "Is Mona involved in any of this?" she finally asked.

"Central to it, although I take full responsibility for my actions."

"What actions?"

His breath came out in one slow shudder. "There's no other place to begin but at the beginning."

"I'm waiting." The determination in her eyes softened at his misery.

"I met Mona one night in the emergency room. She was waiting for her father to finish his rounds and wandered in dripping with glamour and wealth. She captivated me. It wasn't hard, considering my background. The struggle to make it through college and med school left me little opportunity to experience the world she traveled in. When she pursued me, I proved an easy conquest."

Brad stood up and walked toward the windows looking out on the busy street below. He drew the curtains, shutting out the scene, as if he wished he could shut out the memories of the past. Resolutely, he paced back and forth, then sat down on the couch again and idly poured more hot chocolate in Laura's cup.

The fragrance of the rich cinnamon-flavored cocoa permeated the air, but Laura pushed the cup aside, her throat closing at the very thought of it. Brad picked up the cup and raised it to his mouth, remembering her lips had touched it last. When he had finished it, he continued.

"I thought I loved her, begged her to marry me, but she would have none of that. Said I was in no position to marry. She was right. I was a hospital trauma surgeon on a limited income, I could hardly support myself, let alone her. Still, I was crazy about her." He stopped to look at Laura; his eyes asked if he should continue.

Her face grew paler, but her eyes took on a dull resoluteness and she merely nodded for him to continue, not trusting her voice.

"She was like a poison in my blood. I was obsessed with her. I'd lost all sense of judgment, perspective. I was enslaved by my emotions. Can you understand what I mean?" His eyes pleaded.

"No, I wouldn't know." She shook her head. "I've loved only once and it never sank to that level."

"And it never would have. Our love was real," he said quietly.

She shrugged, then commented sadly, "I thought it was."

He flinched, then plowed on. "I lost interest in my work. All that interested me was this elusive pursuit. I did everything in my power to capture her. As a result, I was putty in her hands. I proved a most entertaining toy. For a while.''

''Then what happened?''

''She became engaged to her present husband.''

''That ended your relationship?''

''I wish I could say that it did. But Mona saw no problem with having us both and I didn't have the will to resist. I never gave up the idea that she wouldn't ditch him for me. Finally, one day it all came to a climax. I was on duty at the hospital and she called, demanding that I come to her apartment. I told her I was on duty, but I let her convince me to duck out.''

Laura's eyes widened; fear blazed in them. And he nodded.

''We had just admitted an old homeless man in serious condition. I knew he needed constant attention so I turned him over to a new intern and gave him the number at Mona's apartment without telling who or where it was. He was to call me if he needed me, because I was nearby. I thought I could make it back in case the old man worsened.''

''Did the intern call?''

''Yes.''

''What happened?''

''I didn't answer the phone.''

''And you knew it might be the hospital?''

''I knew it was the hospital—I saw the number on her caller ID.''

''Even then you didn't answer?'' Her eyes told him she couldn't believe what her ears were hearing.

''No, I didn't.''

"You just didn't answer it?"

"Mona and I were having a heated argument when it rang. When I touched the phone she grabbed the receiver and slammed it back into the cradle, telling me that if I went back to the hospital, it would be over for us."

"And you didn't respond to the phone?" Laura asked, still not able to accept what he was saying.

Brad put his head into his hands, unable to look at her. "I didn't answer nor did I call back. In fact, I didn't return to the hospital for another two hours."

"And the old man?" she whispered.

"He died." He shuddered. "I'll see his sunken, bloodshot eyes until the day I die."

"Oh, Brad." Laura reached out toward him and touched his hand.

He flinched. "That's not all." He groaned, then looked at her with tormented eyes.

"What—what else could there be?" she stammered, afraid for him to go on.

"I lied about the intern. I said I never received a call."

"Why?"

"In our hospital, an intern is required to call in a physician in case of an emergency."

"And he couldn't get anyone else?"

"He didn't have time. The old man went into cardiac arrest and he was trying to save his life."

"And his procedure?"

"The same one I would have used. Evidently, there was nothing anyone could do. But because a death was involved the hospital had to make an official report.''

''What happened to the young man?''

''The hospital dismissed him for negligence.''

''And you never did anything about it?''

''I tried, but there again I allowed this madness to rule my actions.''

''How could you?''

''Don't you think I know how unfit I am to practice medicine? That I valued human life so little I abandoned my responsibilities to fulfill my own desperate desires? That I ruined the career of a promising young man?''

''I'm sorry. It's just hard for me to take in.''

''How could you understand? You have a set of values, a faith that dictates your decisions even when your emotions rebel. All I had ruling me was my own madness.''

''What madness?''

''My obsession with Mona and what life with her would be like.''

Laura shuddered and closed her eyes, trying to wipe the smiling, cold face of Mona out of her mind.

Brad continued. ''I let Mona convince me to let the incident drop because she planned to propose to her father that he take me into his practice as a partner. Do you know what that meant?''

''Guaranteed financial success, social acceptance and maybe...'' Laura began but couldn't utter the words, her stomach churned and she thought she was going to be sick.

Brad stared at her, his eyes taking in the revulsion

in hers. "Yes, and maybe marriage to Mona. I tried to convince myself her arguments were right. I kept telling myself no one could have saved the old man, that I had not ruined a young man's life and most of all that I, as her father's partner, would be acceptable to her as a husband."

Tears streamed down Laura's face as a thousand emotions fought to gain control.

Brad shook his head sadly. "I was wrong on all counts. Your dad taught me that any living soul is precious no matter what his station in life. I know that somewhere in this world a young man is disillusioned and perhaps has given up medicine because of me. As a side note that you already know, Mona married her wheeler-dealer."

"But she wanted to continue seeing you, as well."

Shame flamed his face. "That's right. But this time I resisted. It was one thing when she was single, but once she was married...well, even I had qualms about that. I had also discovered a certain amount of consolation in the power and prestige my new position had brought me. That's when I planned to marry Darlene. I thought it would be a good business move, while her beauty and polish would add to my image."

"What about love?"

"What I knew about love proved anything but appealing. I determined an unemotional attachment was the only safe venue."

"If you truly put Mona behind you, why were you on your way to Virginia?"

"When Mona heard I was engaged to Darlene, she called and threatened to reveal the truth and ruin me if I didn't come. I panicked and took off in dangerous weather."

"Things hardly seem much different now. You still came running at her first call." Laura's tone had a bite to it.

"You're wrong there." Brad took her hands in his. She stiffened and leaned away from him, the image of Mona burning in her mind. "She's no longer a madness burning in my blood. I see her for what she is and what I felt for what it was."

"Which was?"

"Lust and nothing else."

"Lust?"

"For power, prestige, money and beauty—physical, superficial beauty, that is. Ugly as it is, I've faced it. It was my own weakness, not Mona's influence, that caused me to fail. Now I must pick up the pieces of my life and face the consequences. Then I can begin anew."

"What are your plans?"

"Resign from my practice, go to the hospital board and confess what I did. I will search for the young man I wronged and try to make restitution."

Laura sucked in her breath, her eyes wide, fearful. "Do you know what that means?"

"Yes, at the most I'll lose my license to practice medicine—at the least I'll get a public reprimand. Either way my career is over."

"And you've told Mona?" Hope wrestled with despair on her face.

He smiled, relief easing the lines in his face. "Not yet."

"Oh," Laura whispered, the glimmer of hope extinguished.

He saw it and explained. "Until I met you, I didn't know what I would do."

"Met me?"

"You reminded me that worldly success is not worth losing my soul."

"You're willing to pay the price now?"

He nodded. "Whatever the cost."

"What will you do with everything you've worked for gone?"

"Losing my career means nothing to me. The humiliation of knowing I failed as a physician is a heavy burden, but even that pales in comparison to my losing you. You are my very heart and soul. I shall love you until the last breath I breathe."

She dropped her eyes from his, contrasting emotions rioting within her. He was right. How could she still love him? He was not the Brad she knew and had loved. His past was soiled, his future uncertain. Disillusionment filled her and her heart ached.

She looked up at him, the battle waging within her written in the lines of her body, the contours of her jaw, the set of her mouth, the fire in her eyes. "Brad, I wish I could…"

"I didn't tell you this in order to win you back. Darling, believe me, my motive was pure."

She turned to him; afraid to trust her voice, she whispered, "Your motive?"

"I wanted you to know why I left you—because I loved you truly, rather than that I had taken your love lightly. I can only imagine the pain I have caused you tonight, but maybe it will serve as a release that will allow your tomorrows to begin—a future without me."

She shuddered and dropped her head. A vision of all her tomorrows without him loomed bleak. Yet how could she forget the past and forgive him?

He leaned toward her again and in his eyes she could see sad sincerity mingled with shame. "Your dad was right. Mark Harrod is the man for you. I stood in the shadows and watched you. He loves you, and he deserves you. I dipped from his cup of happiness an impossible dream. Now I'm returning it to him."

Brad suddenly stood up, bent over and kissed Laura on the top of her hair. He walked to the door and opened it, then turned toward her once more.

She looked up, her eyes wide and moist, her full pink lips parted, but no words would come, no encouragement to stay.

His expression grew dark as his eyes devoured her for one last time, then he said, "Goodbye, my darling." And for the second time, he walked out of her life.

Chapter Fifteen

Mark cast a furtive glance toward Laura. Her face appeared even paler than it had the night before and dark circles beneath her eyes evidenced her lack of sleep. She stared resolutely at the road ahead and to the mountains beyond.

"Laura, I don't want to intrude, but would you let me help you?"

"Brad came to my room last night," she replied, peering off into the distance, her voice dull.

"You don't appear to have resolved your differences," Mark observed quietly.

"It may interest you to know that when he left, he gave me back to you." She looked at him then, cynicism sharpening her voice.

"I didn't realize I ever had you. Did I, Laura?" For a moment pain flashed in his eyes, then it was gone.

"Perhaps not in the way you wanted, Mark. We've

always been friends, and if Brad hadn't arrived on the scene, things might have been different, given more time.''

''But he did and nothing has changed, has it?'' Now it was Mark's turn for his voice to dull.

''Some things have.''

''What?''

''I value our relationship more.''

Mark raised a quizzical brow toward her, waiting for her explanation.

''I've learned to appreciate the strong qualities that make you the man you are,'' she said simply.

''And I have Brad to thank for that?'' he asked, an edge to his voice.

''In a way. He told me the real reason he left me.''

''And so I win your admiration by default?'' Mark's jaw clenched as he fought his own emotions.

''Aren't you interested in why he left me?''

''Was it the glamorous Mona?'' Mark spat out, an uncustomary harshness in his usually smooth voice.

''She had a lot to do with it.'' Laura dropped her eyes, her voice so soft he had to strain to hear.

''Can't he decide between the two of you?''

''He said he still loves me. That he will always.'' Her voice broke and she lifted her hand, palms up, in a helpless gesture.

''Yet he gave you back to me?'' Mark queried, his brows drawn together.

''He thinks I belong with you.''

''Where do you think you belong?'' Mark inquired gently, a strange light in his eyes.

''I don't know.''

"Where do you want to belong?"

"Right now just somewhere safe, a protected harbor."

"Like me?"

"You've always been a haven for me."

A sign ahead announced a nearby state park and Mark hit the brake hard, changed lanes and headed down the exit. Laura watched him, puzzled. He stopped the car at an overlook above a clear, tumbling stream.

They both stared at the lovely scene before them without seeing it. Hesitant to speak, they groped for the right words, then Mark turned to her; his usually merry eyes took on an intense light. Taking her cold hands in his, he spoke, choosing his words with care.

"There's no denying it. You have been special to me since that first day in the hospital when you swept into your dad's office straight from med school. I've had to be content to be your friend, your playmate and now your safe harbor. But at some point in time that will no longer be enough for me. Moreover, when your wounds heal, it won't be enough for you. I think you should know that before you say any more."

She shook her head, not wanting to hear his words. Unable to deal with her emotions, she turned her face from him.

"Brad Jeremiah can't just arbitrarily decide to whom you belong," Mark continued, then took her chin between this fingers and turned her face to his once more, looking deeply into her eyes, silently seeking the truth. "Only you have that right, and you must use both your heart and your head when you make your decision.''

He held her gaze, demanding the truth, and in the end she whispered, ''You're everything in a man that a woman could want...''

''Yet it's Brad you want.''

''After last night, I'm not so sure.''

''Why don't you tell me about last night. Maybe together we can make some sense out of his noble gesture.''

''I don't think it was just a noble gesture. I believe he was sincere.''

''Based on?''

''What he told me, the look on his face. When he walked out of that room last night, I believe he walked out of my life.'' She dropped her face into her hands, trembling.

Mark's warm brown eyes turned black as he struggled with his own conflicting emotions. Then he sighed, gained control, moved across the seat to her and gathered her against him. ''Maybe not. Perhaps he just wanted your reassurance that you would take him back.''

''Oh, Mark.'' She shuddered, then poured out the whole sordid story of Brad's involvement with Mona.

The color drained from Mark's face as he listened. When she finished, a heavy silence settled around them. He seemed at a loss for words. Then he murmured, ''Passion's price is high.''

''You think his career is ruined?'' she asked. Fear widened her eyes as they searched Mark's for some sign of hope in his. She found none.

"Except for a miracle, the debonair Dr. Jeremiah has lost everything." Sarcasm laced Mark's voice.

"That's what he said." Laura nodded; her shoulders sagged in defeat.

"What's his attitude?"

"He's resigned to the consequences. He thinks he deserves them."

"Well, he does. But then, if we all got what we really deserve, need I say where we would all end up?"

"You're excusing him?" Laura asked, shocked at Mark's response.

"Not at all, but I can put myself in his place and pity him."

"How could you? You would have never done that!"

"Thank you for your vote of confidence, but given the right circumstances, who knows what any man might do? Love is a powerful force. I can understand how it could obsess a man until his actions were irrational."

"He said it wasn't love."

"What did he call it?"

"Lust."

"A powerful, destructive force," Mark added.

"And he's destroyed?" she said, her lips trembling.

"If he's lost you, then truly he is destroyed." Both pain and understanding struggled within Mark.

And Laura knew that Mark was no longer talking about Brad Jeremiah.

* * *

An early snowfall lightly blanketed the mountain hamlet and Christmas carols floated across the crisp night air from a small chapel in the valley just below. Without warning a deep yearning to go home gripped Laura's heart and she turned her little car toward the mountain and her parents' house. Tonight Mark would say she needed a safe harbor. And she did.

Her mother's smile sent a warm welcome straight to Laura's battered heart and her father's hug soothed the loneliness that had too often haunted her of late. Unaccustomed to the sensation, she had filled her hours with work, but tonight work and even Jonah could not cover the aloneness the festive season seemed to magnify inside her.

After returning from Louisville, she had increased her hours at the hospital, and occasionally, she would take her father's old reliable Land Rover and make the trek up into the mountains alone. The experience proved a balm to her battered heart as she reveled in the creative medicine she had to practice in primitive circumstances.

Laura tried to push thoughts of Brad from her mind, but even a brief respite proved a conduit for painful memories. When she held a newborn baby in her arms, one she had just assisted into the world, the past came tumbling back and she wondered what he was doing. She wondered if he had found the courage to follow through on his promises.

Tonight Laura snuggled into the soft, supple leather chair in front of the roaring fire, issued a contented sigh and tried to shut down her memory and relish the moment. The glow from the fire, and a cup of cider, warmed the core of coldness that had seemed her constant companion of late.

A knowing look passed between her parents and her mother asked casually, her voice gentle and encouraging, "Laura, we don't mean to pry, but wouldn't you like to tell us about your trip to Louisville?"

Laura stood and walked toward the fireplace. She placed her cup carefully on the mantel and leaned against it, enjoying the heat of the fire as it turned her cheeks pink. Then, with a deep sigh, she turned to her parents.

"It's past time that I told you about what's happening in my life. I know you and Jonah have been worried, but I've been reluctant for a lot of reasons to talk to you. Most of all I've had to sort my own feelings out, and I hated to do anything to make you think less of Brad."

"Humph!" David growled. "How could we think much of a young man who just up and left without a word to anyone? I guess he told you he was going?"

"He told me and…" She hesitated. "I saw him in Louisville."

"Why did he leave, Laura?" David pressed impatiently.

"When an old, uh, friend of his, showed up at our door, his memory came crashing back and with it any future that we might have had together."

"You had made some plans toward a shared future?" Cassie chose her words carefully.

"I thought I loved him."

"Thought?" Cassie gently probed.

"The man I loved was not the same man who left."

"Laura, begin at the beginning. Tell us the whole story. We want to understand. We want to help," Cassie said.

Tears filled Laura's eyes as she looked into the loving and concerned faces focused on her. She shuddered and, haltingly at first, then as if the dam had burst, recounted the story of her love and Brad's past.

"And that's the state of my love life." Laura sighed, adding, "Now it's just a matter of a new beginning and allowing the healing process to do its work."

"And it will, darling. God will see to it," her mother said encouragingly, tears brightening her own eyes.

Laura looked at her mother and sighed again. "I cling to the truth that my life is not purposeless and try to accept that what has happened is all part of God's plan. However, for the present it's difficult to see how any good could come from it."

David patted Laura's hand and spoke, his voice gentle. "What Brad did was not part of God's plan. That was his own weakness and poor judgment. Your involvement in it is another matter."

"Meanwhile, how do I cope?" Laura asked, a smile trembling around her lips, a question in her eyes.

"You just step out one day at a time, Laura, trusting God to bring the future into focus in His good timing. That's what faith is all about. Believing God has our good in mind, especially when we can't see evidence and don't understand what's happening in our lives.''

"I'm trying to, Dad. It's just so hard to keep my feelings from overcoming my faith.''

The winter proved harsh and sickness came to the mountains. The staff at the hospital worked feverishly to save the old and the young from the ravages of influenza and pneumonia.

Ice and snow hindered David's visit to his mountain patients and he forbade Laura to venture out alone while the roads and trails remained treacherous. Many nights Cassie McBride paced the floor, sleepless with worry because her husband had insisted he couldn't abandon his patients.

Tonight proved more difficult than all the rest combined. Darkness cloaked the sky with a heavy blanket, smothering the twinkling light of the heavens. The wind whipped around the turrets, hurling sleet like miniature missiles against the windows. A loud gust shook the house and Cassie walked to the window to peer out for the hundredth time. The clock struck four and she had had no word from David. He had left in the cold darkness of yesterday morning with a warm kiss from her and a promise from him to return before nightfall. Now it was twenty-three hours later.

She pulled her robe close around her, shivering even while the crackling fire radiated warmth into the room. The lights flickered and fear fought for control. Then the lights stabilized and she let out her breath, but still her heart raced and worry etched her brow.

Perspiration beaded her brow, while the rest of her

shivered. Her mind ran rampant with possibilities. A smile trembled about her lips as she thought of her husband, his devotion to his work, to his God. Where did common sense come into play? Her smile broadened. Never when it collided with his vision. She'd learned long ago, that if she would be David's wife and their marriage succeeded, she must share his vision.

And oh, how she had tried. But sometimes, at midnight and he was away from her side, she ventured close to the precipice and considered the risks. When she did, she came face-to-face with the horror of what life would be without him. It was during those rare moments that circumstances obscured the vision and she knew real fear. Tonight the wind howled, the sleet pelted down and her heart failed her.

What was that? A noise like something scratching at the door riveted her attention. She belted her robe and picked up a flashlight and ran through the house to the kitchen door leading to the porch.

She opened it, and the cold north wind jerked it from her hands and slammed it against the wall, dislodging a print of a tranquil mountain scene. It crashed to the floor, scattering slivers of glass across the kitchen. Cassie hardly noticed as she leaned into the wind and walked toward the porch steps. Snowdrifts now crusted with ice rested against the porch; a thin powder had blown through the screen and dusted the floor. Her foot slipped, but she kept her balance as she shone her flashlight out the screen door. Her light rested on a dark mound at the bottom of the steps.

"David!" she breathed, more in prayer than exclamation. In a flash, she slipped and slid to his side. Kneeling in the snow beside him, she never felt the cold wetness that soaked her robe; her only awareness was the tall broad frame of her husband, unmoving in the deepening snow.

Mark's grave face expressed more than words could as Cassie searched it for some sign of encouragement. She recognized none and, stoically, dropped her head, her own face wooden. Jonah stood at the window as if he could see through the winter darkness, ignoring Mark's presence, while Laura lingered behind, giving one last look into the room before she faced her mother's questions. Neither she nor Mark had any answers, and they wouldn't for twenty-four hours.

Cassie moved over on the utilitarian sofa of bilious green plastic and chrome legs to make room for the younger doctor. Her mind irrelevantly noted the ugly furnishings and she thought how inconsiderate the hospital had been to furnish an intensive care waiting room so uncomfortably. She focused her attention on something she could control, and vowed she would remedy the situation as soon as possible.

She hardly heard Mark telling her that it would be twenty-four hours before they knew if David would live, and even longer before they would know if he had suffered any permanent disabilities. A coma still gripped him, and none of them could say how long he'd been exposed to the weather or how far he had walked. If Cassie had not heard him, he would not have survived more than a few minutes longer. Now they were concerned with the complication of pneumonia.

"Cassie, look at me," Mark commanded, recognizing her reaction as denial.

She turned her large, liquid brown eyes, dark circles beneath them, to him. "Yes, Mark?"

"Did you hear what I said?"

She shook her head. "You don't know what you're talking about. He's going to be all right. No matter what you said."

"He is a strong and vigorous man, but you have to understand he is very ill. I know you can handle the truth," Mark stated.

"Truth? What do you know about the truth, Mark Harrod?" Cassie cried.

"I just told you the truth," Mark whispered, pained.

"No, the truth is I won't even consider having to go on without him. I have wanted nothing more for the past thirty-three years than to walk with him, to talk with him, to love him and to share his life, and that's all I want for the rest of my life. He will not abandon me now."

Mark threw a helpless look toward Jonah, who had retreated from his vigil at the window to hear Mark's assessment. The old giant with silver hair and sad blue eyes pulled a chair up beside Cassie and took both her hands in his. "Little one, we can't promise you that our David will survive or not. What Mark is trying to do is prepare you for the long, hard road ahead."

Cassie jerked her hands away from Jonah's. "One without, David? You can't know what you're telling me."

Jonah's eyes held Cassie's, as he waited for sanity to return to his daughter-in-law. "More than anyone in the room, I know, my dear."

Then memory flooded Cassie and she hurled herself into the arms of the man who had become more of a father to her than her own. "Oh, Papa, I'm sorry. You above all know the terror I feel."

"Yes, my dear, and I can promise you, whatever happens you will have the strength to endure."

"Without David? Never!" She shuddered.

"Your strength doesn't come from David. And the One who can give it has promised that He will never forsake you."

Cassie shuddered. "Then why do I feel so frightened and alone right now?"

"Perhaps because you've been demanding instead of asking," Jonah gently suggested.

Laura sat by David's bedside, her heart constricting with his every labored breath. It had been twenty-four hours and there had been no improvement in his condition. At times she thought he had roused when she spoke to him, but his vital signs revealed it had been more wishful thinking on her part than fact. Now she bathed his parched lips, trying to give him comfort.

Not only was she worried about her father, but she also felt that her mother's reaction to the situation warranted careful observation. Cassie's robust color had turned pale, her skin translucent. It wouldn't do if she became ill.

So Laura sat ministering to her dad, worrying about her mother and feeling more parent than child to her parents. A grim smile parted her face as she felt empathy with all those family members who had suffered the illnesses and loss of loved ones. She knew that whatever the outcome of this painful episode, she would be a better, more compassionate, doctor because of it.

What a pity that pain was such an inevitable part of the learning process. And then she thought of Brad for the first time in days. She marveled that her heart failed to lurch, but rather, with a sad interest, she questioned his whereabouts and wondered how he was doing.

David groaned, bringing Laura's thoughts to the moment at hand. And she lamented that it took one severe problem to put another in perspective.

For over a week David lingered between life and death. Cassie stayed glued to his side, but peace had replaced panic in her and Laura breathed a sigh of relief. When the patient proved restless, her mother had only to lay a gentle hand on his chest and whisper to him, and it calmed him.

His heart stabilized, encouraging Mark and Laura. He was too weak to ascertain what damage it had sustained, but they had another problem. Pneumonia had developed in both lungs and it refused to respond to typical treatment.

Mark had reservations about Laura's increasing the

dosage of antibiotic but had no alternate suggestion, so they went forward, only to see the patient's fever rise to a fearful height. At any moment, the two doctors dreaded another cardiac distress, but his heart held steady. They kept Cassie and Jonah informed of every decision and the two of them remained as steady as a rock; Cassie's former behavior was a mere memory.

On the fourth day David's fever climbed higher and his restlessness grew to an alarming level. No sedative proved effective, and not even Cassie's calming presence seemed to reach him. Mark and Laura recognized that his chances of making it through the night grew dimmer by the hour. Unless they found something the pneumonia would respond to, they would lose him.

Laura, exhausted from her constant vigil, found her own emotional control eroding. Trained as a physician to administer healing, she had proven powerless to help her father. Mark looked across the bed toward her, took in her pale, drawn features—and curtly ordered her from the room.

Laura, miffed at Mark's command, whirled from the bed and, grabbing her heavy jacket, marched down the hall toward the front exit of the hospital. She paused beside her little red car, then turned and headed for the gorge. The wintry weather had let up. As sometimes happens in February, a false spring teased the countryside; the ice and snowstorm of the week before were only a memory, except for the bits of ice lingering in shadowy places where the sun never shone.

She pulled her coat tight around her and jogged along the rim of the gorge. Before long, the tension that had bound her eased and the gentle wind seemed to blow the cobwebs from her mind. She had to agree; Mark had proven right again. She had needed the fresh air, to get away for a moment.

She paused in a sunny cove shielded from the wind and sat down on a rock. Inevitably, her thoughts returned to her dad's room and the dilemma they faced. Never had she felt so helpless and so aware that the healing process transcended the hands of a doctor. While she could medicate and do procedures, only God could direct the body's responses. And her heart and soul cried out, begging for wisdom and for healing to begin in her father. Tears of frustration and surrender trickled down her face; she tasted the salt on her lips, as she admitted the physicians had reached the limit of their knowledge. They knew nothing else to do.

Emotionally spent, she gave in to the drowsiness that overtook her in the warm sunlight. She leaned against a broad tree trunk and nodded off, exhaustion finally having its say. Disturbing dreams of her father lying deathly ill, interspersed with dreams of him robust and hearty, teaching a class on his experiments with lung disease, denied her a restful respite. Instead, she awoke with a start, an urgency to return to the hospital propelling her toward the dim room where her father lay hooked to systems supporting his very life.

One glance at Mark's face and she knew the news was not good. The young doctor looked up at her, relief in his eyes at her return. He gave some quiet instructions to Gretchen, then motioned for Laura to follow him out.

"I'm so glad you're back. He has worsened. Nothing we're doing seems to be effective, and we're going to lose him unless we can come up with something else immediately."

Fear caused Laura's heart to race as she whispered, "Do you have any suggestions?"

Mark smiled, softening the worry that lined his face. "Strange that you asked. Fifteen minutes ago I would have said no, but I suddenly thought about the unique procedure your dad has used with a few miners whose lung disease refused to respond to treatment."

"And?" Laura asked breathlessly.

"I don't know if it has ever been used for pneumonia, but I think we ought to try it. Believe me, we have nothing to lose."

"It's as bad as that?"

"As bad as it can be, Laura. I've got to tell your mom."

"No, try the procedure first."

"But we need permission and to prepare her."

"It'll work," Laura assured him.

"It's a long chance, that's all."

"Trust me. It's not a long chance. It's what you're supposed to do. Get busy—we're wasting time," Laura commanded.

Mark looked at her, confusion wrinkling his brow, "Okay, you're the boss."

Laura chuckled. "I believe you just ordered me out because you were the boss."

He rolled his eyes, his broad shoulders sagging with fatigue. "We'll go into that later."

"I don't know anything about the procedure. Do you?" Laura asked as an afterthought.

"I have detailed instructions written by the big guy and I've assisted. You'll have to assist."

"As long as I don't have to hold you up. You look like you're about ready to drop."

"I'll be fine if this works."

"Don't even say 'if,'" Laura commanded.

Mark watched the IV, waiting impatiently for it to empty. It was the third of four, and as yet David showed no sign of rallying. He was no worse in the past hour, but neither had he improved.

Laura watched her dad and monitored his vital signs, while Cassie stood at his bedside, his limp hand in hers. They had told her they were trying an experimental procedure and that his condition had worsened. Laura's mother never flinched but encouraged them to attempt whatever they thought would be best; now she wiped his brow and leaned over to kiss him.

Gretchen changed the IV bottle and Mark increased its speed, knowing they fought the clock for David's survival. When the bottle reached the three-quarters mark, David stirred. Large beads of perspiration broke out on his forehead. Cassie tenderly wiped them away with a towel, then caressed his cheek with a cool hand. He turned his head toward her and her fingers brushed his parched lips.

Slowly, two blue eyes opened like narrow slits and he whispered her name.

"I'm right here, darling." Cassie spoke softly; her eyes sought Mark's, questioning.

"And I've been far away." His voice was no more than a husky murmur.

"But you've come back, my love," Cassie responded, bending down to him, as tears flowed down her cheeks and bathed his face.

David's progress proved slow. Without him, the hospital staff staggered under a heavy workload. Mark worked night and day, as did Laura, to fill the gap, but the more they worked, the more they seemed to get behind.

One morning, whistling a merry tune, Mark met Laura on her rounds.

"And what do we owe this good humor to, Dr. Harrod?" Laura asked, amusement sparkling in her eyes.

"A day off, I think."

Laura stopped short and placed her hands on her hips, "How do you rate that?"

He laughed, a glimpse of the old Mark peeking through. "Simple, I'm the boss."

"I thought the boss wasn't supposed to have any time off."

"Maybe I'm a new kind of boss," he drawled. "Let the peons do all the work."

"Yeah, right. I see how you let all of us do all the work." Laura laughed. "Seriously, I'm glad you're taking a night off. I was beginning to fear we had lost our old Mark under a pile of responsibilities.''

"Would you have missed him?" Mark quizzed, his tone light but his eyes serious.

"In the worst kind of way," Laura admitted.

"I'm glad," he commented.

"Tell me how are you're celebrating such an auspicious occasion?"

"I'll have to admit, it's a little bit of business and, I hope, a lot of pleasure."

"Oh?" Laura asked, her curiosity pricked.

"Several months ago I promised to take Gretchen to a show in Louisville that she had tickets for. I had forgotten all about it until she reminded me Monday. So I thought we'd drive in early and I'd look up this doctor who might be interested in coming on staff here."

"How did you find out about him?"

"Giles suggested he might be interested."

"Fat chance any of those Louisville doctors would be interested in any low-paying position we might have to offer."

"Guess it depends."

"Depends on what?"

"Why he's a doctor, I reckon."

"Well, good luck. To say we need some help would be an understatement."

"You can say that again. I never realized the load David was carrying. I'm surprised he hadn't collapsed a long time before now."

"And you're going to be in the same boat, Dr. Mark."

"No, not me. If there is one thing I've discovered since David's illness, it's that an administrative job is not for me. I'm a doctor, maybe a research doctor, but no administrator."

"Then what will we do? Dad cannot go back to what he was doing."

"You're absolutely right. That scare we had with his heart should be a warning to him. But who knows? Maybe this guy will be just the one we need."

"That would be nothing more than a miracle, considering Louisville and our pay scale."

"We've already seen one miracle this month, Laura. Maybe God is ready to give us another," Mark reminded her earnestly, all traces of frivolity gone.

"When you put it like that, Mark, I can't wait to see the outcome," she responded, hope blossoming.

Chapter Sixteen

Laura hurried down the corridor, head down; she had overslept and now she was late for a staff meeting.

She slipped into her chair, trying to press her unruly locks into order. Her folder crashed to the floor, spilling its contents beneath her chair. She looked up from the floor to find eight pairs of eyes trained on her. She lifted her hands in a helpless gesture and remarked, "Haven't you ever had a bad-hair day?"

The room exploded with laughter as Mark called the meeting to order. After giving an update on David's improving condition and reading the financial statement, he recognized Ray Giles's raised hand.

"Let's get to the real business at hand, Harrod. What about that help you promised us?" Dr. Giles drawled. "It's not that I'm complaining, but my family think they need to see me more than once every two weeks before midnight."

"How about looking at your agenda, Giles? That

issue is the next item for discussion," Mark responded curtly.

Laura interrupted, "Have you found someone, Mark?"

"Yes, I have." The young doctor nodded; an uneasy light struggled with determination in his eyes.

"Tell us about him, Mark," Dr. Giles said encouragingly, his levity turned sober.

"I interviewed a candidate, felt his skills were exactly what we needed, and then I discussed it with David. With his approval I hired the man on a ninety-day trial basis."

"When will he be here? In all seriousness, we're ready for a little relief." Ray sighed.

"How about now?" Mark asked with an infectious grin, and moved to the door and opened it.

Broad shoulders filled the doorway and glowing black eyes searched the faces around the table, before finally resting on Laura. Her eyes widened in surprise, then the color drained from her face as her lips soundlessly formed one word; "Brad."

"What in the world are you thinking about, Mark? How could you do me this way? You didn't even warn me," she all but shouted.

"I wasn't sure he was coming until last night, and you were in surgery. Besides, it wouldn't have changed anything."

"I thought you were my friend, and now you have betrayed me," Laura accused through clenched teeth, her whole body trembling with anger.

"I did what I thought best for the hospital, for David and for you,'' Mark explained when she finally stopped for a breath.

"And who gave you the right to decide what is best for me?"

"You didn't give me permission, but you did involve me. Putting that aside, however, I'm asking you to separate your personal and professional life. Who better than you knows that we have reached a crisis situation here in the hospital? It is vital for your father's full recovery that we resolve it.''

"Brad's not going to relieve your crisis, because if he stays, I leave. Then you and I both know you will have big problems,'' Laura threatened.

"You're talking foolish.''

"How in the name of common sense do you expect me to work with him? After what I told you, why would you even want him?''

"The same reason you still want him,'' Mark said, his words hurled like missiles across the small office.

"You don't know what you're talking about!''

"I do, and that's one of the reasons he's here.''

"And what about us, Mark?''

"There never was an 'us' and any chance there might have been ended on Clingham's Bluff last spring on a foggy, stormy afternoon. We've both waited too long to face it.''

"He's not the man I fell in love with.'' Laura closed her eyes, trying to shut out the present, to quell the memories that bombarded her.

"He's even more than the man you fell in love with.''

"What would you know of that?'' she jerked open

her eyes and demanded.

"I knew him then and I know him now."

"How?"

Mark crossed the room and took her by the shoulders, shaking her gently, his expression somber. "I'd rather he told you."

"I don't want to talk to him." She twisted away.

"Why?"

"In the past I was too vulnerable to his effect on me. I won't let that happen again." Her words found their way through clenched teeth. "Maybe he's just too charming."

"Brad is much more than charm," Mark disputed.

"You're a strange champion for him, Dr. Harrod." Bitterness glittered in Laura's eyes.

Mark looked at her hard, impatience replacing compassion. "Do you know where I found him?"

"Some swanky restaurant with Mona on his arm?" Laura asked, her tone biting.

"No, in a rescue mission, treating drunks and addicts."

Her eyes widened; her voice silenced. She shook her head as if to clear it.

Mark nodded. "That's right. He lives there. Gave up his high-rise apartment, moved into the mission and went on staff of a local mission society."

"What happened to his job?"

"When he told Mona he was going to the hospital board to confess the whole sordid mess, that was the end of his cushiony practice," Mark said.

"Did he lose his license?" she asked, afraid to hear the answer.

"No. The hospital didn't wish to make a public issue of it, so they censured him. However, when he attempted to find the young man that he had wronged, they gave him a stern warning to drop the issue."

"And did he?"

"No, that's when he and the hospital parted company."

"That explains the rescue mission work," Laura remarked dryly. "I guess that's all he could find."

"Not quite. He had already been working three nights a week at the mission on a voluntary basis. When his practice fell through, he went on full-time for a small salary and a place to live."

"But he was eager to give it all up and come here?"

"No. He made his decision only a couple of days ago."

"Was he reluctant because of how I might react?"

"You did enter into the decision, but only because your being here was too strong a personal pull."

"Oh?"

"He had to make sure it was the right professional move."

"And what decided him?"

"He found the young man he had wronged. It seems he was well established in a flourishing practice on the south side of town, working out of another hospital. He held no grudge against Brad. When he heard what Brad was doing at the mission, he paid a visit there and was so impressed he offered half his staff on a volunteer basis. With the time donated, the mission no longer needed a paid staff, so the way was clear for Brad to come here. Now only one obstacle remains. You.''

"What about Dad?''

"He is perfectly at peace with the decision.''

"How could he be?''

"Because Brad is an excellent doctor, committed to what we are doing here, and to the best of his ability made amends for his mistakes. Give me a good reason the hospital shouldn't give him a second chance,'' Mark declared.

Mark's insistence collided with a wall of silence. Finally, Laura shrugged, staring stonily into his eyes. "I can't think of one at the moment.''

The lanky doctor towered over Laura, his mouth a rigid line, as he searched her face, looking for a solution. Then he lifted her chin gently. His eyes softened as he asked, "Can you give me a good reason that Laura can't give him a second chance?''

"You of all people are asking me why?'' Laura said; her voice rose in frustration.

"I'm asking you to examine your heart to understand your feelings.''

"And why should I?'' she demanded, irritated with his pressing.

"Because only then will you be able to go on with your life,'' Mark explained, patience in his voice, a painful wisdom in his somber eyes.

"I don't need Brad Jeremiah to go on with my life,'' Laura shot back angrily.

"Life is more than just a day-to-day existence, my dear.'' Mark reached out and caressed her cheek tenderly.

Laura dropped her head, unwilling for Mark to see the painful truth he'd uncovered.

"I told you, Mark, I don't know what I think or feel." She was desperate for him to let her slip back into her shell, where life could go on without her painful involvement.

But Mark refused to let her escape. He continued. "Did his revelations make a difference in the way you feel about him?"

"How could they not?" Her voice rose a decibel, as she battled for control.

"Face the truth about yourself, Laura," he insisted sadly.

"And that is?" She looked up into his face, surprise overtaking the pain.

"You haven't forgiven him." His smile softened the harshness of his words.

Horror overtook her as the truth of what Mark had just said dawned on her. "You mean, I can't forgive Brad?"

Mark didn't respond, only continued to look deeply into her eyes, forcing her to come to her own conclusion.

Laura pushed away from him and took in a deep ragged breath, then nodded. "You may be right. I don't know that I would be willing to take him back, realizing what he has done."

"Even if he is truly sorry and tries to make restitution?"

"How could he make restitution for what went on between Mona and him?"

"No restitution can be made for that. Only forgiveness can be given. That episode had nothing to do with you. That happened before Laura.''

"Then why is it every time I close my eyes I see her with him?"

Mark chuckled. "That's jealousy, my dear."

Laura shuddered and looked up at Mark. A solitary tear trickled down one cheek. "Not a very pretty picture of myself, Dr. Harrod."

"When we face ourselves as we really are, it never is," Mark said as he lifted a strand of hair tenderly from her face.

"But necessary?"

He nodded. "Especially when it stands in the way of our happiness."

"And you think happiness is a possibility?"

"It can be, but both your and Brad's future happiness depends on the choice you make."

"My choice?" She wrinkled her nose, confused.

"Whether you choose to forgive or not," Mark reminded her, a sad smile turning up one corner of his mouth.

"We're back to that, are we?" Laura pulled away from him.

"That's the only place to begin." Mark sighed, growing visibly weary with her resistance to the truth.

"You're saying I need Brad to be happy?" she countered defensively.

"No, you need to forgive Brad before either of you can find happiness."

"Same thing," she argued.

"Not at all. It is our response and attitude toward a situation that determine our happiness, not the situation." Mark reached for her, pulling her around to face him.

"Then how do I forgive?" She asked, her voice just above a whisper.

"The same way you found the strength to go on without Brad."

A touch of defiance threaded her voice, still not quite willing to accept what Mark said. "If God wants me to forgive Brad then why hasn't He helped me before now?"

"Perhaps because you haven't asked." Mark looked down, an impatient frown wrinkling his smooth brow.

"And if I ask?" A tremulous smile played around her lips.

"'Ask and you shall receive'," he quoted. Relief relaxed his face as he saw the dawn of acceptance in the troubled blue eyes that held his.

Then Laura laid her head on his shoulder and he cradled her in the curve of his arm. Both stood silent for a moment. Surrendering the last vestige of her defenses, she relaxed in his arms. When she looked up into his eyes, hers gleamed bright and clear for the first time in months. With an unacknowledged acceptance of what he said, she asked in a husky voice, "What made you so wise, my good and dear friend?"

He smiled with his crooked grin, "Life, and— love."

"Oh, Mark, what about your happiness?"

He looked at her long and hard, as if memorizing her beautiful face. Then he replied, "I've learned that my happiness is not dependent on having or not having you.''

Overcome for a moment by the powerful emotions she saw in his expression, Laura could say nothing. Instead, she stood on tiptoe, slipped her arms around his neck and embraced him, planting a kiss on his cheek.

Mark gathered her close, and as she buried her face in his neck she heard him whisper, ''Goodbye, my love.''

Seconds passed as they stood in each other's arms, their eyes closed. Both appeared reluctant to end the embrace and with it a chapter of their lives. Engrossed in the moment, they failed to hear the office door widen, nor did they see the pain flare in the dark eyes that watched the tender scene.

Brad silently deposited the chart in his hand on Mark's desk and turned toward the door. Laura's eyes flew open, only to rest on his two broad shoulders retreating through the doorway. When Brad turned for one last look, his eyes collided with Laura's.

A cynical smile twisted his mouth as she hastily pushed away from Mark. ''Somehow I always knew that's where you belonged.''

''Brad, you don't understand,'' Laura protested.

But he was gone.

A late-season influenza epidemic assisted Brad in his determination to avoid Laura. Every doctor did double duty, and he had little time to think about anything but the demands of the moment. Only when he went to his sparsely furnished room to sleep at night did the memory of her in Mark's arms descend to haunt him. Occasionally, when they had met in the hall, she would speak and a few times pause as if she had something more to say, but he would rush on, not ready to hear the words he knew she had waiting for him.

He never questioned the rightness of his decision to return to the Blue Ridge hamlet, only how he would find the strength to work and live so near her when she belonged to someone else. He considered it punishment he deserved, but nothing helped the deep yearning that gnawed inside him.

On the day Brad arrived, he visited David's room to make his peace with him. He found an acceptance from the father that he knew would never be forthcoming from the daughter, and his heart grieved. The older McBrides, both father and mother, proved the soul of encouragement, but even they offered no hope where Laura was concerned. In fact, they never mentioned Laura.

Brad felt his burden lighten after his encounter with David, for he sincerely desired his approval. Now he was free to strive for it. As far as his career goals were concerned, for the first time since medical school he felt that his life was on target. So he sought to mitigate the dull, throbbing pain in his personal life with work.

It took Brad only a few days to validate the wisdom of bringing him on staff. He worked hard and long hours. His skill and knowledge unquestioned, he assumed more and more responsibilities.

Mark gradually turned over administrative duties to

Brad that he abhored and found him doing them well and in half the time. Although Brad's manner with the patients seemed abrupt at times, compared with Mark's warm demeanor, his competence inspired confidence.

Brad's relationship with Mark proved cordial and professional, but neither mentioned the scene that Brad had interrupted in Mark's office the day he had arrived. While Laura sorted out her emotions, she failed to address the issue. Each day that passed without an explanation or resolution, their polar positions solidified a chasm between them that grew more difficult to bridge with any measure of understanding.

Brad eased his body down into an armchair on the patio outside the doctor's lounge. He was bone weary. For twenty-one days straight he had pulled sixteen-hour shifts without a break. While his mind relished the schedule, his body had begun to object. He knew he would have to take a break or else his mental capacity would suffer. No doctor could afford not to be sharp when life and death decisions were his to make.

But what would he do with a day off? Sleep? How did Shakespeare so aptly put it? "To sleep was perchance to dream." How could he bear the dreams? He could scarcely bear the reality of Laura so near, yet beyond his reaches.

Mark had been kind and had scheduled their work so that they rarely saw each other. Yet every time Brad got a glimpse of her golden hair in the distance, his heart raced, his arms ached to hold her and his mind replayed the scene of her in Harrod's embrace.

He knew he had only himself to blame for what had happened. But that hardly made it any easier to bear. What was a man to do? He was as lovesick as if he were a young whelp of a boy. Disgusted with himself, he walked to the railing and peered up into the mountains.

What a majestic sight they proved, garlanded in evergreens, a blue haze caressing the crevices and peaks then drifting down to kiss the rolling hills beneath.

His mind tripped back to the morning that he had surprised Laura with a picnic hamper. He remembered how he had watched her while she swam at the waterfall. His eyes had feasted on her beauty, while his heart had stirred with strange exhilarating emotions. Even yet he could feel her in his arms, the sweetness of her lips, how it felt when her fingertips had stroked his cheek.

The fragrance of her hair as it whipped across his face was as real as it had been so many months ago. He dropped his head, closing his eyes, and gripped the railing until his knuckles turned white. A deep shudder ripped his insides and exited in a growl from deep in his throat.

A light touch on his shoulder jerked him around. He was angry and embarrassed that someone had dared disturb his private moment, had uncovered his despair. The fragrance of her still burned in his mind and he sorrowed at turning loose his dream. He shook himself as if from a trance when he came face-to-face with his fantasy, the fragrance real, not imagined.

Laura spoke softly, questioningly. "Brad?" Concern filled her, for she had seen the look on his face. His torment frightened her. "Are you all right?"

"Yes," he answered tersely, turning from her and releasing the railing but balling his hand into a fist.

"What's wrong?" she asked, alarm growing in her.

When he looked down at her, harshness burned in his eyes and threaded his voice, making him a stranger to her. He growled more than spoke.

"Don't you know?"

"It looks too serious to play a guessing game. Perhaps you'd better tell me. Is it a patient?" she inquired, gently, encouraging him the way she would a distraught child.

His laugh contained no mirth, only pain. "No, my dear, it's not a patient."

"Well, then, what is it?" She stood so close to him the scent of her perfume filled his nostrils, and then a breeze wafted strains of her golden hair across his face and he groaned.

Laura reached out and touched his face; dismay lined her own. "Whatever it is, Brad, you can work it out."

He grabbed her hand and jerked it from him. "What I'm feeling I can never work out."

"I thought things were going quite well here for you. Mark and Dad couldn't be more pleased."

He nodded like someone awakening from a nightmare. "That's gratifying."

"Then tell me, what happened?"

"What happened?" He threw back his head and laughed, but only pain and bitterness were in his eyes.

Her expression questioned, but this time she waited.

He leaned in toward her and pointed his finger. "You are what happened to me. Dr. Laura McBride walked into my life, wrapped her fingers around my heart and hasn't let go."

"Oh, my dear. Am I the reason for your agony? Forgive me." Compassion brightened her eyes with unshed tears.

"No, I alone am the reason for my agony. All I can see when I close my eyes is your loveliness wrapped in the arms of Mark Harrod. The pain of regret is difficult to bear when I know that what could have been mine now belongs to him."

Laura flinched; her chin rose in defiance as she took in what he said. "You are mistaken, Dr. Jeremiah. I belong to no one on this earth, not you, not Mark."

Brad's pain was nudged aside as hope flared in his heart.

She continued, "I am the one who will decide whom I want. It is not your privilege to decide who is best for me, nor is it Mark's responsibility. I am not the prize in some game of toss between the two of you. I am an adult woman, gifted, skilled and able with God's direction to make the decisions I need to make, especially concerning whom I love and want to spend the rest of my life with."

"You mean, you and Mark aren't...? But I saw you in his arms."

"No Mark and I aren't involved, nor do we have any plans beyond friendship. What you saw and what you interpreted it to be were two entirely different things.''

''All I can say is that was the most tender expression of friendship I've ever witnessed,'' Brad growled, afraid to believe what he had heard.

''Intruded on, you mean,'' she responded, her tone biting.

''His door was not closed, Laura. How did I know what was going on behind it?'' Brad snapped.

''Must you make it sound so sordid?''

'''Sordid' was not quite the word I would use to define it.'' Pain reignited in him at the memory.

''If not, how would you define it?'' Anger and embarrassment flushed her face.

''As the end of all my dreams.'' His voice fell to almost a whisper, his dark eyes baring his very soul.

''Oh, Brad.'' She shuddered, feeling his pain. She took a tentative step toward him, forcing herself to confront him, but wanting to escape from the agony she encountered in him. ''Don't you know that you can't place your dreams in a person? You'll find only disillusionment when you do.''

''You could never disappoint me, Laura.''

''I already have. Just look at you, the pain in your eyes, the defeat in every line of your body. People let one another down, Brad.''

''The way I let you down?'' he asked quietly, moving even closer to her, his arms rigid at his side, his hands balled into tight fists as he struggled not to touch her, not to take her in his arms.

''As I allowed you to,'' she admitted, her head up.

"You're taking responsibility for what I did to you?" he asked, not comprehending.

"We are responsible for how we respond. That's why I can be neither the end nor the beginning of your dreams, Brad."

"But you are. Without you there is nothing of value left."

"You are of value, your dreams, your destiny. The pursuit of them must not depend on anyone else."

"But you gave them to me. You showed me a better way, the way to a more productive life," he disputed.

"Perhaps God allowed me to shed some light along the way, but I am not the way. Your destiny depends not on me but on the dream God gave you and your choice to fulfill it."

"And what about your dreams, your destiny, Laura?"

"Through the pain of these last months, God has shown me my weakness and His strength. I needed that before I could fulfill the dream he had put in my heart."

"Needed?" he asked, puzzled.

She nodded and smiled sadly. "It proved a necessity for my survival."

He winced and backed away from her and sat on the railing suspended over the valley beneath. With the majestic mountains behind him, he looked long and deeply into her eyes. When he failed to find the light of encouragement he searched for, he asked, his voice dull, "What proved necessary?"

"I had to realize that life must go on in the face

of disappointment and heartbreak. I've learned that my destiny rests not on the actions or reactions of someone else but in my own responses. And more than that, when I proved inadequate to fulfill the dream, it was His strength that sustained me and kept me moving forward.''

''So you have need of no one?'' he asked, defeat written on his face and in his slumping shoulders.

''You misunderstand. We all need someone, but not to blame for our failures and disappointments, nor to set our course.''

''What about someone to walk along beside, to share in the pursuit and the joys of accomplishment?'' he insisted, a moment of encouragement strengthening his voice.

''If God grants a person that privilege, they are blessed indeed,'' she said tenderly.

''Has He, Laura?'' he asked almost fearfully.

''Perhaps.'' Her smiled broadened.

''And it's not Mark?'' A spark of hope ignited, struggling with disbelief.

''No, it's not Mark,'' she replied quietly; her eyes, now glowing, held his.

''Then who?'' He stepped toward her, his heart in his eyes.

Her smile broadened. ''Who indeed?''

''Dare I even hope for your forgiveness and friendship someday?'' he queried, a tentative smile curving his mouth.

''Oh, my darling, Brad, you have my forgiveness now, but friendship seems such an inadequate word to describe what I feel for you.'' Laura's gaze wrapped him in a warm, loving light, her whole face illumined by an inner glow.

Brad breached the space between them in one swift stride and crushed her in his embrace. His lips found hers and all the heartache and uncertainty of the past months dissipated in the warm response of her embrace and willing lips.

When he finally lifted his head, he whispered, "I've come home at last."

Laura reached up and pulled his head back to her and murmured against his lips as she nestled deeper into his embrace, "We both have, darling."

* * * * *

Dear Reader,

Somewhere deep within the heart of every woman is a longing for romance, for that special someone in whom she can safely invest her dreams and to whom, without reserve, she can give herself mind, body and soul. Yet in a time when marriage failures have reached astronomical proportions and love is defined as whatever feels good between two people, is it any wonder that many have lost hope of ever achieving a lasting and meaningful relationship based on trust and commitment?

I am convinced that amid the wreckage, there is a hope that goes unrecognized because it lies within the parameters of God's guidelines for love and the expression of it. Because I have experienced the excitement and joy of romantic love as God meant it to be, I am dedicated to writing wholesome and exciting love stories that encourage women not to settle for something less than what God has intended for them.

Some of you may have lost hope and may be tottering on the brink of compromise. You can relate to the explosive feelings and temptations my heroine, Dr. Laura McBride, experiences in *A Healing Love*. However, it is my prayer that her strong commitment to her values will inspire you to stand firm and wait. For those of you who have found God's answer in the field of romance, may her story bring a sweet remembrance of the excitement and the ultimate bliss of resolution God's way. May it inspire you to a renewed appreciation for what God has so richly blessed you with and a commitment to guard it.

Deria Staton English